MARY ANNE AND TOO MANY BABIES

Logan and I carried our stuff to the lobby, threw away our rubbish, and struggled into our coats. Logan picked up Sammie's basket.

"*I'm* supposed to have her tonight!" I cried.

"No way. You almost lost her," said Logan. "Not that I really want to take care of her *again*. I'm always taking care of her."

"You mean you're always *taking* her. You never let me have her."

"Okay, then *you* take her tonight."

"Oh, no. You don't trust me. You just said so."

Logan didn't answer. He grabbed Sammie's basket. Then he went off to call his parents for a lift home, and I called my dad, and Logan and I went off in a huff.

Is Mary Anne re~~ady~~ to marry Logan, *and* become a paren~~t~~ ~~babys~~itters will have to wait an

Also in the Babysitters Club series:

Kristy's Great Idea
Claudia and the Phantom Phone Calls
The Truth About Stacey
Mary Anne Saves the Day
Dawn and the Impossible Three
Kristy's Big Day
Claudia and Mean Janine
Boy-Crazy Stacey
The Ghost at Dawn's House
Logan Likes Mary Anne!
Kristy and the Snobs
Claudia and the New Girl
Goodbye Stacey, Goodbye
Hello, Mallory
Little Miss Stoneybrook . . . and Dawn
Jessi's Secret Language
Mary Anne's Bad-Luck Mystery
Stacey's Mistake
Claudia and the Bad Joke
Kristy and the Walking Disaster
Mallory and the Trouble with Twins
Jessi Ramsey, Pet-Sitter
Dawn on the Coast
Kristy and the Mother's Day Surprise
Mary Anne and the Search for Tigger
Claudia and the Sad Goodbye
Jessi and the Superbrat
Welcome Back, Stacey!
Mallory and the Mystery Diary
Mary Anne and the Great Romance
Dawn's Wicked Stepsister
Kristy and the Secret of Susan
Claudia and the Great Search
Mary Anne and Too Many Boys
Stacey and the Mystery of Stoneybrook
Jessi's Babysitter
Dawn and the Older Boy
Kristy and the Mystery Admirer
Poor Mallory!
Claudia and the Middle School Mystery
Mary Anne vs. Logan
Jessi and the Dance School Phantom
Stacey's Emergency
Dawn and the Big Sleepover
Kristy and the Baby Parade
Mary Anne Misses Logan

Mallory on Strike
Jessi's Wish
Claudia and the Genius of Elm Street
Dawn's Big Date
Stacey's Ex-Best Friend

Look out for:
Kristy for President

Babysitters Specials:
Babysitters on Board!
Babysitters' Summer Holiday
Babysitters' Winter Holiday
Babysitters' Island Adventure
California Girls!
New York, New York!
Snowbound
Babysitters at Shadow Lake
Starring the Babysitters Club
Sea City, Here We Come

Scholastic Children's Books,
Scholastic Publications Ltd,
7–9 Pratt Street, London NW1 0AE, UK

Scholastic Inc.,
555 Broadway, New York, NY 10012-3999, USA

Scholastic Canada Ltd,
123 Newkirk Road, Richmond Hill,
Ontario, Canada L4C 3G5

Ashton Scholastic Pty Ltd,
P O Box 579, Gosford, New South Wales,
Australia

Ashton Scholastic Ltd,
Private Bag 92801, Penrose, Auckland,
New Zealand

First published in the US by Scholastic Inc., 1992
First published in the UK by Scholastic Children's Books, 1994

ISBN 0 590 55589 8

Typeset in Plantin by Contour Typesetters, Southall, London
Printed by Cox & Wyman Ltd, Reading, Berks.

10 9 8 7 6 5 4 3 2 1

MARY ANNE AND
TOO MANY BABIES

Ann M. Martin

Hippo

This book is for Alice,
my friend from around the world

1st CHAPTER

I was thirteen years old before I became a sister, and guess what? My new sister was my age, thirteen. Were we long-lost twins, separated at birth and reunited thirteen years later? No. Although that's much more interesting than the truth. The truth is that my sister is actually my stepsister. Earlier this year, my father got married again, and he happened to marry the mother of Dawn Schafer, who was already one of my best friends. So Dawn and I went from being best friends to being best friends *and* sisters. Not many kids are that lucky.

My name is Mary Anne Spier. I'm an eighth-grader at Stoneybrook Middle School (commonly known as SMS) in Stoneybrook, Connecticut. I was born here and have lived here all my life. Before Dawn came along, I had a very small family. Two people. My dad and me. Of course, I had a

1

mum in the beginning, but she died when I was really small. I don't even remember her. After she died, Dad brought me up. He did a good job, even if he was strict, but I always wished for a bigger family; at the very least for a baby brother or sister.

When I was twelve and in the seventh grade, a new family moved to Stoneybrook—Dawn and Jeff Schafer and their mother. The Schafers had just been divorced, and Mrs Schafer wanted to bring up her kids in the town in which she'd grown up. That town was Stoneybrook. Unfortunately for Dawn and Jeff, *they* had grown up in California, so the move to cold, snowy Connecticut was something of a shock to them. Dawn was determined to make the best of things, though, and she adjusted to her new life fairly quickly. For one thing, she made new friends straight away. I was her first friend, and I introduced her to my friends in the Babysitters Club, which is a business we run. (I'll explain that later.) Straight away, Dawn and I started spending a lot of time at one another's houses, and guess what we discovered one day when we were looking through our parents' high school yearbooks. We found out that a long time ago my dad had dated her mum. They'd been sweethearts. But then they graduated from high school, and Dawn's mother went off to college in

California and met Mr Schafer and married him and then had Dawn and Jeff. Meanwhile, my dad had also got married, although he'd remained in Stoneybrook.

Well, Dawn and I knew just what to do with our secret. We arranged for our parents to meet again, and after a while they began going out together, then *finally* they got married. (In case you're wondering, Jeff moved back to California to live with his father. That happened before his mum married my dad. He was simply never happy in Connecticut. He missed his old life too much. I love Jeff, but I hardly ever see him.)

"Dawn? How come the hedge clippers are in the bread bin?" I asked one day. It was a Monday afternoon. School was over, and Dawn and I were prowling around the kitchen, making a snack.

Dawn shrugged. "Mum's responsible, I'm sure. I'll put them back."

Dawn took the clippers from me and headed for the door to the garage. She was smiling.

Dawn's mother, whom she calls Mum and I call Sharon, is just a teensy bit, oh, scatterbrained. Sharon is really nice, and I'm lucky she's my stepmother, but I'm just not *used* to finding hedge clippers in the bread bin, or my sweater in the freezer, or the TV remote control on a shelf in the bathroom. I grew up with a father who could have run for the presidency of the Neat People's Society. Dawn grew up with a mother who wouldn't have been allowed within miles of a meeting of the NPS. Actually, she isn't so much messy as she is completely disorganized—as opposed to my father, who colour-codes his socks. How they became friends is beyond me. How they became husband and wife is, I think, beyond even *them*, but they do love each other. And the four of us are learning how to live together without going batty. A few months ago, I might have freaked out if I'd found a pair of hedge clippers in the bread bin. Now I can handle the situation calmly.

Dawn came back from the garage, and we sat at the kitchen table with snacks in front of us. Mine was a nice, normal after-school snack—an apple and a handful of chocolate chip cookies. Dawn's was a salad bar—a carrot, some celery sticks, a radish, a little square of tofu, and a small container of uncooked peas. This is an example of the difference between Dawn and me, and between her mum and my dad. Dad and I eat the kind of food we were brought up on, a little of everything—fruits, vegetables, dairy stuff, meat, sweets. Dawn and her mum think it's practically a crime to eat meat. Or sugar. A really great dessert for Dawn is something like, some berries. Now, I am not, I repeat *not*, addicted to junk food the way our friend Claudia Kishi is, but excuse me, berries are not dessert as far as I'm concerned. Cake is dessert. Chocolate mousse is dessert. A large brownie is dessert. *Maybe* berries are dessert, but only if a piece of cheesecake is underneath them.

Dawn poked around at her peas, and I bit into my apple.

"I saw the twins' baby brother this morning," said Dawn. (We have friends— not close friends, just school friends—who are twins. Their names are Mariah and Miranda Shillaber, and they have a brother who is just a year and a half old.)

"You did?" I said. "Where? Is he adorable?"

"Yeah, he's pretty cute. He was with Mrs Shillaber. They'd dropped off Mariah and Miranda at school."

"The twins are so lucky," I said. "I wish our parents would have a baby. They still could, you know. It isn't too late."

"And if my mum doesn't want to give *birth* to another baby," added Dawn, "then she and Richard could adopt one." (Richard is my father.)

"I know. It worked for Kristy's family."

The parents of one of our close friends, Kristy Thomas (who's also a member of the Babysitters Club), adopted a two-and-a-half-year-old Vietnamese girl. And they already had six kids between them.

"My mother wouldn't even have to give up work," said Dawn. "Kristy's mother still works. Of course, her grandmother lives there now."

"Yeah. I'm not sure we could convince a grandparent to pack up and move in with us. A baby *is* sort of a big job."

"I suppose so. But who could take better care of a baby than *us*? We're expert sitters, after all. I mean, we do belong to the Babysitters Club."

"By the way, what time is it?" I asked.

"Four-thirty. Our meeting won't start for an hour."

"Okay. I just don't want to be late. You know Kristy."

Dawn rolled her eyes. She knew all right.

We went back to our snacks. After a few moments, Dawn said, "Do you *believe* that new course we have to take? Instead of career class?"

"What? Modern Living?" I replied.

"Yes! I've never heard of such a thing. We're going to learn about marriage and job hunting and family finances? And *divorce*! I think I already know enough about divorce, thank you."

"I suppose it is pretty weird. At least Logan will be in my class." Not to brag or anything, but Logan Bruno is my boyfriend. We've been going out together for a pretty long time—even though we have definitely had our ups and downs. I'm the only member of the Babysitters Club to have a *steady* boyfriend. If you knew Logan you'd understand why I like him. He's kind and caring and funny. He's really gentle, but he also plays great baseball and football. He's good-looking, too.

"My class tutor," Dawn spoke up, "said we have to take Modern Living because—and this is a direct quote—'it's important that we explore and experience the realities of being an adult in today's changing society.'"

"That sounds like an introduction to a really bad social studies video," I said.

Dawn giggled. "I don't think it's fair that only the eighth-graders are subjected to this torture. Don't the sixth- and seventh-graders need to know how to be adults, too?"

"Yes," I answered, "but they'll get their turns when they reach the eighth grade."

I finished the last of my cookies, swept the crumbs off the table, and stood up. Dawn cleared away our serviettes. (Her mother may be messy, but Dawn is neat and organized.)

"We'd better go," said Dawn.

"Okay. Oh, I have to feed Tigger first!" Tigger is my grey, tiger-striped kitten. When Dad and I moved out of our house and into the old farmhouse Dawn's mum had bought, Tigger came with us. He's our only pet. I love him to bits. (I think Sharon

7

is still getting used to him. I don't know what's taking her so long. He's absolutely adorable.)

I scooped up some cat biscuits into Tigger's dish. Dawn looked at her watch again. "Now we'd *really* better go," she said.

"Okay. I'm ready." My sister and I left for Claudia Kishi's house.

2nd CHAPTER

I still feel a little funny riding my bike to Claud's. That's because I used to live just across the road from her. Riding my bike from one side of the street to the other would have been sort of silly. But my new house isn't nearby. I can still run inside the Kishis' house without bothering to ring the bell, though. Kristy and I did that when we were little. (Kristy also used to live opposite Claud, next door to me, but she's moved, too.) And we continue to do it. So do the rest of the members of the Babysitters Club (or BSC).

Dawn and I dashed upstairs and raced past the door of Claud's older sister, Janine the Genius. She wasn't there, though. Then we ran into Claudia's room, picked our way over the junk on her floor, and flopped onto her bed. I was pleased to see that we were not the last club members to arrive.

"Hi, everyone," Dawn greeted Claudia, Kristy, and Jessi Ramsey.

"Hi," they replied. (If we didn't sound overly enthusiastic, remember that we'd seen each other at school just a couple of hours earlier.)

Kristy Thomas was sitting in Claudia's director's chair, her visor perched on her head, a pencil stuck behind one ear.

Kristy is the chairman. (Of the BSC, I mean.)

Jessi, one of our junior officers, was leafing through the club notebook.

As I found a comfortable position on the bed, I glanced at Kristy. She was staring at Claud's digital clock. That clock is the official club timekeeper, and when the numbers flip from 5:29 to 5:30, Kristy begins a meeting, whether all the club members are present or not.

I suppose Kristy has a right to do that. After all, she's not just the club chairman, she's the person who started the BSC. The club was her idea. What is the BSC? It's really a business, and a successful one. This is how it works. Three times a week—on Mondays, Wednesdays, and Fridays, from five-thirty until six—my friends and I gather in Claud's room and wait for parents needing babysitters to call us. When a call comes in, one of us agrees to take on the job. This is great for parents. They make one phone call and reach seven people, seven

10

expert babysitters. So they're bound to line up a sitter quickly. They don't have to phone one person after another, trying to find someone available.

How do parents know when to phone us? How do they know when we hold our meetings? Because we advertise—you know, leaflets and posters. Also because we've been in business for a while now. We have a good reputation.

Anyway, Kristy is the chairman, since she started the BSC. She is overflowing with fantastic ideas. Kristy is the one who thought of keeping a club notebook, which is like a diary. Each time one of us finishes a sitting job, we're supposed to write about it in the book. Then, once a week, we read through the recent entries to find out what happened on our friends' jobs. This has turned out to be really helpful.

Kristy also came up with the idea for Kid-Kits. Every member of the club has made a Kid-Kit. A Kid-Kit is a large box that has been painted, decorated, and filled with child-centred things—our old games, books, and toys, art materials, activity books, and so forth. Our sitting charges just love to see us show up with our Kid-Kits. They may have the most spectacular toys ever created, but show them something new (even if it's old, it's new to the kids),

11

and suddenly it's more interesting than anything they've got themselves. Somehow Kristy knew that.

Kristy seems to be a natural with kids. She certainly spends enough time with them at her own house, although for a long time only one of her brothers and sisters was younger than she was. Hmm—that's pretty confusing. What I mean is, Kristy's mum got remarried just like my dad, and when that happened, her family changed. A lot. When Kristy and I used to live next door to each other, her family consisted of her two older brothers, Sam and Charlie; her little brother, David Michael; and her mum. Her dad had walked out when David Michael was just a baby. Several years later, her mum began seeing this guy Watson Brewer, who happens to be a millionaire. He also happens to be divorced, the father of two little kids. After Mrs Thomas and Watson Brewer got married, the Thomases moved to the other side of town into Watson's mansion. That was when Kristy's family began to grow. The Brewers adopted Emily Michelle, a little girl from Vietnam. Nannie, Kristy's grandmother, moved in to help look after her. And, Watson's children, Karen and Andrew, live at their father's every other weekend. Also, they acquired a dog and two goldfish, and Watson already owned a cat.

Did I tell you that Kristy is my other best friend? Actually, she's my first best friend, since we grew up together, and I didn't meet Dawn until the middle of the seventh grade. A lot of people think Kristy and I make a pretty weird duo. That's because we're so different. Kristy is extremely outgoing and is known for her big mouth. (Well, she is.) Also, she loves sports and even coaches a softball team for little kids. (Her team is called Kristy's Krushers!) I, on the other hand, am shy. I'm whatever you call the opposite of outgoing. (Ingoing? Ingrown?) I think before I speak. I'm romantic (maybe that's why I ended up with a steady boyfriend before any of the other BSC members did), I cry easily (nobody likes to go to the cinema with me), and I do *not* enjoy sports. However, Kristy and I look sort of alike. Everyone says so. Our faces are the same shape, we both have brown hair and brown eyes, and we're short for thirteen. We dress differently, though. Kristy's happiest when she can just drag on a pair of jeans, a poloneck, a sweatshirt, her trainers, and maybe a baseball cap. (Her uniform.) She never bothers with jewellery or make-up. (Well, hardly ever.) I wear clothes that are a little more trendy—as trendy as my dad will allow me to look. Mostly, I suppose I dress on the casual side. I don't have pierced ears (neither does

Kristy), but I do wear jewellery, including clip-on earrings. And I experiment with my hair sometimes. Nothing way out, though. So Kristy and I are quite different. Maybe that's why we've been such good friends. We complement each other, personality-wise.

You know who's the opposite of us in almost every way? Claudia. Yet she's a good friend, too. We voted Claud as the vice-chairman of the BSC. We thought that was fair, considering we meet in her room three times a week, mess it up (usually), take over her phone, and eat her junk food. The phone—that's another reason we hold our meetings in her room. Claud has not only her own extension, but her very own phone number. That means that when job calls come in, we don't tie up someone else's line, just Claud's. You may think Claudia's job isn't difficult. I know it sounds like that, until you realize that not everyone remembers to call the BSC during our meetings. When parents call during off-hours, Claud has to deal with those jobs.

In what ways is Claud different from Kristy and me? All right, let me see. First, she comes from a smaller, less complicated family. It consists of her parents and Janine. No pets. And Claud's interests are art, junk food, mysteries, babysitting, and fashion, although probably not in that order.

14

Claudia is a fantastic artist, and she's addicted to junk food and Nancy Drew mysteries. Chocolate, crisps, and books are hidden all over her room. (They're hidden because her parents disapprove of both addictions. They wish she would eat healthy food and read the classics.)

Claud is also very fashion conscious, unlike Kristy and me. To begin with, she's exotic-looking. No brown hair and brown eyes for her. Claud is Japanese-American. Her hair is jet black, long, and silky. Her dark eyes are almond-shaped. Her skin is creamy and clear (despite the junk food she consumes). She loves experimenting with her hair, plaiting it, twisting it up, wearing ribbons and hair slides and ornaments in it. And her clothes are outrageous. Her parents let her dress in whatever style she likes. A typical Claudia outfit might include a sequinned shirt, ski pants (maybe black), low black boots, dangly turquoise earrings, and ribbons woven through tiny braids in her hair. And she wouldn't forget sparkly nail varnish.

Another thing about Claud. She's a *terrible* pupil. She could be a good one if she tried, but school doesn't interest her. Sometimes her awful spelling drives me crazy—but I love her anyway.

"Hi, everyone!"

"Hey, Stace!" we replied.

Stacey McGill had dashed into club headquarters, followed closely by Mallory Pike. They had arrived *just* in time. As soon as they had sat down (Mal on the floor with Jessi; Stacey backwards in the desk chair), Kristy announced, "This meeting of the Babysitters Club will now come to order. Any important business?"

"Subs day!" cried Stacey. She's the treasurer, and one of her jobs is to collect subs from the seven main club members every Monday. (Two more people belong to the club, but they do not attend meetings and don't have to pay subs. They're associate members, kids we can call on to babysit if a BSC call comes in and none of us can take the job. Guess what. One of the associate members is . . . Logan!) Anyway, Stace is great at maths, so she's the perfect choice for keeping track of the money in our treasury, which is a brown envelope. We use the money to cover our expenses: to help Claudia pay her phone bill, to buy new items to replace used-up ones in the Kid-Kits, and so forth.

Like Claud, Stacey is a real fashion freak. She dresses wildly, wears lots of jewellery (her ears are pierced; so are Claudia's), and her mum lets her get her blonde hair permed. Stacey grew up in New York City. In fact, like Dawn, she didn't move to Stoneybrook until the seventh grade.

Recently, her parents got divorced, which has been hard on Stace. Now she lives with her mum, while her dad is back in NYC. Stacey has no brothers or sisters. Also no pets. She's funny, outgoing, caring, wonderful with children, and a teensy bit boy crazy. I really admire Stacey. She's been through a lot, and her troubles seem to make her a stronger person. Apart from the divorce, Stacey has to cope with a medical problem. She has a disease called diabetes. Her body can't break down sugar the way most people's bodies can, so she has to monitor her diet extra carefully (no sweets or desserts), test her blood several times each day, and (this is the gross part) give *herself* injections of insulin. Even so, Stacey ends up in hospital from time to time, but she always bounces back and is usually pretty cheerful.

What happens if Stacey or one of the other club officers has to miss a meeting? No problem. Dawn takes over for that person. As alternate officer, that's her job. She has to know everything about running the club, but that's easy for Dawn Schafer, since she's almost as organized and neat as my father is.

Dawn is also very much an individual, which is one of the reasons she became the second of my two best friends. I like her independence, even though I eventually learned that individuality plus independence does not necessarily equal self-confidence. Dawn has some chinks in her armour just like everyone else. In general, though, she's easygoing and not likely to be swayed by what other people are doing or thinking.

Dawn has the most amazing hair I have ever seen. It's at least as long as Claud's, just as silky, but as light as Claud's is dark. It's nearly white, sort of the colour of sweet-corn. Dawn's eyes are blue and sparkly, she's tall and thin, and her clothes are as individual as her personality is. She wears what she feels like wearing and manages to look both trendy and casual at the same time. Her mum is not at all strict about what Dawn wears—which may explain why Dawn's ears are double-pierced, so she can wear two pairs of earrings at the same time, although she often wears four non-matching earrings!

Dawn, Kristy, Claudia, Stacey, and I are eighth-graders at SMS. The other two main members are eleven-year-old sixth-graders at SMS. They are Jessi Ramsey and Mallory Pike, our junior officers. "Junior" just means that their parents will allow them to babysit only after school or at weekends; not at night unless they're sitting for their own brothers and sisters. Mal and Jessi are another pair of best friends, and I can see

18

why they're drawn together. Each is the oldest kid in her family: Jessi has a younger sister and a baby brother, and Mal has *seven* younger sisters and brothers. Each loves kids and is a terrific babysitter. And each feels that her parents treat her like an infant. They *were* finally allowed to have their ears pierced (only one hole per ear, of course), but Mal, who wears glasses, is not permitted to get contact lenses, and both have to dress kind of like . . . oh, like me, for instance. On the tame side.

Mal and Jessi adore reading, especially horse stories, but other than that, their interests are pretty different.

Jessi is a ballet dancer, a good one. She takes lessons at a special dance school in Stamford (the city nearest to Stoneybrook). In the mornings, she wakes up early to practise at the *barre* in her basement, and she has performed in lots of big productions. I think she will be a star one day.

Mal, on the other hand, likes to write and draw. She makes up stories and illustrates them. Also, she keeps journals. I bet she will become a children's book author one day.

In terms of looks, Jessi and Mal are pretty different, too. Jessi's skin is a deep brown, her hair is black, and she has the long legs a dancer needs. Mal is white, her curly hair is red, and she'd give just about anything to get rid of her glasses. Also her brace, even though it's the clear kind and doesn't show up too much.

Ring, ring!

"I'll get it!" cried Claudia.

Stacey had finished collecting the subs, and now the phone was ringing with what was probably our first job call of the day.

Claud grabbed the receiver. "Hello, Babysitters Club." She listened for a moment. "Yes? . . . Oh, hi, Mrs Salem," she said. (We met Mrs Salem when we were taking an infant-care class. She and her husband have twin babies, a boy and a girl.) "Of course," Claud was saying. "Okay, I'll call you back in a few minutes. 'Bye." Claudia hung up the phone and turned to me. "That was Mrs Salem. She needs a sitter for Ricky and Rose next Tuesday afternoon. Who's free?"

I think I forgot to mention that I am the secretary of the BSC. I'm in charge of the club record book. (Guess who thought of keeping a record book.) I write down any important BSC information and I schedule *all* of our jobs.

I looked at the page for the following Tuesday. "Hey, guess what. I'm the only one free," I said. "And I'd *love* to sit for the twins. Babies. I can't wait!"

Claud phoned Mrs Salem to give her the good news.

3rd CHAPTER

"Do you, Mary Anne Spier, take this man to be your husband?"

"I do."

"And do you, Logan Bruno, take this woman to be your wife?"

"I do."

"I now pronounce you man and wife, for as long as you are members of my Modern Living class."

I had never been so embarrassed. It was the second session of Modern Living, and everyone in our class had to pair up and get married. At least Mrs Boyden hadn't asked Logan to kiss me.

Why were we getting married? Good question. I'll give you Mrs Boyden's answer. "Class," she had said during our first session, "you are in the eighth grade. Most of you are thirteen years old now. Some of you are fourteen, a few of you are twelve. Despite how old or young you may feel, the truth is that you are now biologically capable of becoming parents, or you will be soon. How many think you are capable of parenting, of being part of a couple, or of living on your own?"

I didn't know about living on my own or getting married, but I certainly knew a lot about looking after kids.

So I put up my hand.

I didn't realize Mrs Boyden would call on me. I'd thought she was just asking for a show of hands. But she said, "Mary Anne?"

"Yes?" I replied. "Oh. Um, well, I babysit all the time," I said, my face flushing. "I can change nappies and everything."

Mrs Boyden hadn't seemed too impressed. She just nodded. And then she started talking about getting married. "The best way to experience adult life is to live it," she said. "That's why you are going to pair up, get married, and stay married until this class is over. You may choose your partners if you wish. I will assign partners to those pupils who do not choose their own."

Nearby, someone whispered, "As if getting married to someone you see three times a week is realistic."

I glanced at Logan then, who was sitting on my other side. He smiled at me. We were going to "get married." It was an exciting prospect. *I* knew we were ready to take the big step. Well, I thought we were. Okay, I wasn't sure at all, but I definitely wanted to find out. Especially if it meant we could spend more time together.

Our class spent the rest of that first session talking about things like how old our parents were when they got married, and what being married *really* means. I had dared to put up my hand to contribute to the conversation, but only after Shawna Riverson had said, "I think getting married *really* means that you have a plastic bride and groom on your wedding cake, right, not those little bride and groom mice or something. Or maybe you could have a giant plastic wedding bell right, and some bluebirds or something."

The class sniggered, and even Mrs Boyden looked surprised.

Well, after a comment like that, nothing I said could sound any more stupid. So I raised my hand. "I think marriage really means commitment. It means you love your husband or wife so much that when you have a problem, you try to work it out so you can stay together."

"You are definitely on the right track," Mrs Boyden said to me. "Thank you, Mary Anne. Class, there's a little more to marriage than the wedding. That's just the first *day*."

Even so, we had our shot at weddings in the very next session of Modern Living. "Are all of you engaged to be married?" asked Mrs Boyden at the beginning of class.

Four boys put up their hands. "*We* aren't," they said, looking disgusted. And Gordon Brown added, "There are nine girls and thirteen boys in this class, Mrs Boyden. All the girls have been taken."

"We have not been 'taken'!" cried Erica Blumberg. "We are not pieces of property. You can't claim us."

"Okay, okay," said Gordon. "All right, the girls have all been used up."

Erica's face practically turned purple. "We are not hot water, either. We aren't some commodity. You can't use us up."

"Commodity?" I heard Shawna whisper. "Doesn't she mean condiment?" Shawna looked really pleased with herself.

"Okay, okay, kids. Please calm down," said Mrs Boyden, holding her hands in the air. "We'll discuss this some other time. Gordon, you're right. Two of our couples will consist of boys only. Can you deal with that?"

"I am *not* going to be a girl," said Howie Johnson.

"Well, neither am I," said Gordon and the other boys.

"Do they have to decide ahead of time who's the wife and who's the husband?"

asked Logan. "Maybe they could decide later. Maybe they wouldn't even have to tell us their decisions."

Mrs Boyden opened her mouth to say something, but before she could start speaking, Howie said, "Yeah, yeah. We'll decide later."

"Okay," replied our teacher, in that tone of voice grown-ups use when they *mean*, "If that's the way you want it, but I think it's a pretty poor idea. I suppose you'll just have to find out for yourselves."

The girls and the remaining boys had paired up by themselves. Mrs Boyden created two couples out of the other four boys because they refused to do it for themselves. Then the marriage ceremonies began, and soon I was Logan Bruno's wife and he was my husband and I was being silently thankful that we didn't have to kiss in front of our entire Modern Living class, not to mention in front of Mrs Boyden.

"From now on," said our teacher, when the weddings were over, "when you are in class, you will sit together as couples. In fact, when you are in class you will *be* couples, and I'll expect you to think and behave as such. You may be asked to be couples outside class," she added, and her words sounded somehow ominous. (I glanced at my "husband," and he shrugged

25

his shoulders as if to say, "That doesn't make any difference to us. You and I are already a couple.")

Guess what Mrs Boyden assigned us for homework. She asked each couple to get together, discuss money and finances, and decide whether they could be a financially independent couple.

"Huh?" said Shawna. "You mean like really rich?"

"No, not independently wealthy," said Mrs Boyden patiently. "Financially independent. Could you support yourselves? Could you live in your own place and buy groceries and clothes and pay your electricity bill and phone bill and taxes and so forth?"

"Don't all married couples support themselves and pay their bills?" asked Gordon. "Don't all families?"

"No," our teacher replied. "Most do, I suppose, but it doesn't happen by magic. You don't get married and suddenly come into money. So your homework is to work out how you would fare if tomorrow, say, you were married and on your own." She paused, then she smiled and added, "Actually you *are* married and on your own. How are you going to cope?"

Logan and I found out that afternoon. I went to my husband's house as soon as school finished. The house didn't feel like my husband's, though, since my husband's younger brother and sister and mother were also there. Kerry, who's nine, and Hunter, who's five and has terrible allergies, were in the kitchen with us, waiting for Mrs Bruno to take a bag of popcorn out of the microwave.

"Put it idto two bowls, Bubby," said Hunter stuffily to his mother. "If you do't, thed Kerry hogs it. She eats faster thad be."

"I do not!" exclaimed Kerry.

At that moment, the doorbell rang and so did the phone. Mrs Bruno reached for the phone, and Kerry ran for the door.

"Dear," Logan said to me, "I apologize for the noise here today. Let's go and work in the dining room. We can close the doors."

"All right, sweetheart," I answered, grinning.

"Ugh!" cried Hunter. "Dear! Sweetheart! You two sound like you're barried or subthig." He sniffed loudly.

"We are," replied Logan. "Hunter, this is your sister-in-law."

I was eager to get to work. "Come along, darling," I said to Logan.

We closeted ourselves in the dining room. We were equipped for an afternoon of work—newspaper, writing pad, pens, calculator, a packet of biscuits, and a flask of iced tea.

"Let's see," I said, when we'd seated ourselves at the table and spread out our things. "First we'll need a place to live."

"Right." Logan opened the paper to the ads for flats for rent. "We'll have to start small," he said. "We probably won't be able to afford a house straight away. How many bedrooms do you want?"

"I think two will be enough at first. One for us, one for guests."

"Okay . . . two-bedroom flats. Here's one. The rent is . . . oh, my lord, it's two thousand dollars a month!"

"Two *thousand*?" I repeated. "What does the flat come with? Fourteen bathrooms and a private plane?"

"I don't know. Maybe it's in a really posh block. There must be cheaper flats. Or maybe two *thousand* was a misprint. Maybe a zero was added by accident."

But it wasn't a misprint. The rent for the cheapest two-bedroom flat we saw advertised was eight hundred dollars a month.

"We'd have to earn nine thousand, six hundred dollars a year just to pay our *rent*," I said. "How much money do you earn each year, Logan?"

Logan estimated how much money he

earned babysitting and doing odd jobs. I estimated how much money I earned babysitting. We added the figures together. Then we stared at each other with our mouths open.

"We couldn't even pay a month's rent," said Logan.

"Let's look at smaller flats," I suggested. "We could live in a studio flat for a few years. That would be okay."

"Only if we found one that cost about thirty cents a month. Remember, we have to buy food and clothes."

"And pay all those bills and taxes and stuff," I added.

Then Logan said, "Just for laughs, let's turn to the ads and see if there are any really big discounts on at the supermarkets."

There were. But we also saw that steak cost a fortune, even at sale prices. "So we won't eat meat," said Logan. "It's not good for you anyway."

"I don't think we'll eat much of anything," I replied. "Everything is expensive. Even junk food."

"There's just one solution," said Logan.

"What?"

"We'll have to live at home. We are not financially independent."

"Whose home?" I asked.

"Mine. I'm the husband."

"So what? I'm the wife and there's more room at my house."

"But I don't want to live with your dad. He would watch me all the time."

"Well, I don't want to live with my nine-year-old sister-in-law and my five-year-old brother-in-law. Anyway, I want us to have our own place. I want to hang curtains and paint cupboards."

"I don't think they let you do that if you aren't paying rent," said Logan. "We haven't found one of those thirty-cents-a-month places yet."

I sighed. "I know. But there *is* more room at my house."

"Yeah. You're right. Okay. We'll live in your bedroom."

Logan and I wrote up our findings. I knew Logan would be embarrassed to admit in front of the other boys in our class that he'd be living in a girl's bedroom, but that was our only solution. And no matter how silly we found Modern Living, we wanted to do well in the course.

4th CHAPTER

The Salems' house was quiet.

"Ricky and Rose are asleep," said their mother. She sounded quite relieved. Also, she looked sort of tired.

"Is anything wrong?" I asked.

"Oh, not really. It's just, you know, *twins*."

That didn't worry me much. Especially considering that the BSC once sat for fourteen children for a week. And that I've babysat for Mal's brothers and sisters tons of times and even gone on family holidays with the Pikes, as a mother's helper.

I had arrived at the Salems' house for my afternoon babysitting job. School had just finished. I'd gone to my job straight from school. Now I was standing with Mrs Salem in the kitchen.

"All right," she said. "Let's see. The

31

twins will probably wake up in about half an hour. They'll be hungry then. Their bottles are all ready. After they've eaten, you can take them for a walk. The buggy's in the garage. They should probably wear sweaters. The emergency phone numbers are here on the fridge door . . ."

Mrs Salem is so organized. That's one reason my friends and I like to take care of Ricky and Rose. We haven't had too many opportunities, though. The Salems wouldn't let us babysit until the twins reached six months. But now they phone us *fairly* regularly.

Mrs Salem left for her meeting, and I sat at the kitchen table and started on my homework. First I looked over my notes from Modern Living class. We were talking about parenting. I didn't see that it was such a big deal; not for a babysitter anyway. If everyone would just take a child care course, they'd be prepared.

I was opening my maths book when I heard a noise from the first floor. I paused and listened. Definite cooing. I tiptoed upstairs and stopped at the doorway to the bedroom the babies share. Even from out on the landing, I could smell that baby smell—powder and wipes and lotion and clean clothes and wet flannels.

I waited for the sound of tears, but instead I heard only cooing. The babies were talking to each other; at least, that's how it seemed.

"Hi, Rose. Hi, Ricky," I called softly from the landing. I walked into their room quietly. The twins have reached that touchy "fear-of-strangers" phase, and I didn't want to make them cry.

They didn't. The cooing stopped, though. They sat in their cots, watching me solemnly and silently.

"Hey, Ricky. It's me, Mary Anne. I've taken care of you a few times now." I crossed the yellow carpet to Ricky's white cot. I just adore the way the Salems have decorated the twins' nursery. It's bright and airy. Yellow striped curtains hang at the windows. A small shelf is already jammed with picture books. A blue wooden chest of drawers, decorated with a painting of Winnie-the-Pooh, holds most of their toys. Under the window stands the changing table. Around the middle of the wall runs a colourful frieze of teddy bears and balloons.

I didn't approach Ricky too closely yet. Instead, I stepped over to Rose's cot and whispered to her.

"Want to be . . . *tickled*?" I finally said.

Rose's face cracked into a smile. A few teeth showed. I tickled her toes gently. When she began to giggle, I lifted her from her cot and laid her on the changing table.

A lot of babies don't like to be changed,

33

for some reason. I can't understand that. Personally, if I were wearing a wet, smelly nappy, I wouldn't even wait for some-one else to change it. I'd learn to do it myself.

Rose lay on her back and kicked her feet in the air. She let me remove her nappy, which I dropped into the nappy bucket. I know, it sounds old-fashioned. But so what? Mrs Salem does not put disposable nappies on the babies. She found out how bad they are for the environment, and she switched to cloth nappies, even though she and her husband have to wash *loads* of nappies almost every day. They never complain about this.

I pinned Rose into a fresh nappy. Then I looked around the room. "I suppose I'd better dress you in a fresh outfit," I said. From the twins' wardrobe I took a pale blue dress, smocked across the front. I slipped it onto Rose, then completed her outfit—frilly socks and dainty blue cloth shoes. She looked like a princess.

Ricky's turn. He also let me change him without fussing. Then I dressed him in a red-and-white sailor suit. "You look very handsome," I told him.

I carried the twins (one at a time) to the kitchen. I found that I had to plan ahead with the babies. Managing them took some work. For instance, to move them to the kitchen, I had to put Rose back in her cot, carry Ricky downstairs, fasten him in his high chair, return to the bedroom for Rose, then carry *her* downstairs and fasten *her* into *her* high chair. But so what? The babies were as good as gold.

They even gave themselves their bottles. Mr and Mrs Salem must have been pretty happy when the babies learned how to hold onto things.

"Ready for a walk, you two?" I asked.

Ricky smiled at me, and a drop of milk trickled down his chin.

Rose burped, then grinned.

"Charming," I told her, giggling.

I fastened the twins in their double buggy and pushed them down the Salems' drive. If I do say so myself, they looked really cute, sitting side by side, all dressed up, smiling and cooing. I almost wished they were wearing matching outfits so people would know for certain that they were twins, and not just two unrelated babies.

We set off down the pavement. We passed an older woman who paused to smile at Ricky and Rose. Then we met up with a man who stopped to say, "Goodness. Ricky and Rose. You two are certainly getting big. Don't you make a fine-looking pair."

In response, Rose kicked her feet, and Ricky waved his arms around. They gurgled and grinned.

A few minutes later, a couple of little girls flew through the front door of a house and dashed across their lawn. "Hi, Rosie! Hi, Ricky!" they cried. Then they looked at me. "Miss, can we play with the twins, please?" asked the younger girl.

Miss? Honestly, was I getting *that* old? I thought. But what I said was, "Okay, for a few minutes. I'm Mary Anne. I'm babysitting for the twins. What are your names?"

"Sara," said one.

"Bea," said the other.

The girls bent over the babies. They tickled them. They played peek-a-boo and pat-a-cake with them. They exclaimed over their outfits.

"I can't wait until I can babysit," said Bea.

"It's the best job in the world," I replied.

"Is it ever hard?" Sara asked.

"Hard? Nah," I said, completely forgetting about the time Jamie Newton refused to go to sleep, and the day Jenny Prezzioso ran a temperature of 104° and I had to call an ambulance, and the many things that had been broken by Jackie Rodowsky, the Walking Disaster. "It's always fun," I added. "I can't wait until I have children of my own." Or better yet, a baby sister, I thought.

The twins were *angels*," I told Dawn later that afternoon.

It was almost dinnertime. Dad and Sharon had not yet returned from work. Dawn and I had finished tossing a salad and had just stuck a casserole in the oven. It was some vegetarian thing Sharon had concocted. I didn't ask what was in it. I have found that it's better not to know.

"Rose and Ricky are pretty sweet," agreed Dawn.

"They didn't even *cry* today. Not even when I changed them."

"Babies are wonderful."

"I know. I don't understand why Dad and Sharon won't have one. I thought that was supposed to be part of a marriage. Look how badly Watson and Kristy's mum wanted a baby after they got married."

"Would you want a little brother or a little sister?" asked Dawn.

I hesitated. "I know I'm supposed to say I don't care as long as the baby is healthy, but well, I would sort of like another sister," I said. "She would be so much fun to dress up. We could buy her jewellery and hair ribbons and some of those headbands—you know, the stretchy ones."

Dawn sat in a kitchen chair and said dreamily, "What would you want to call our sister . . . or brother?"

"I don't know about a brother, but I

think a beautiful name for a girl is Tara. Or Charity. Or Bea. Isn't Bea cute? I met a little girl today called Bea. Maybe Will would be nice for a boy."

"I think Dawn and Mary Anne are lovely names."

I jumped a mile, then whirled around to see who had spoken. It was Sharon. Dawn and I had been lost in another world, and we hadn't heard our parents come home.

"Are you two talking about babies again?" asked Dad.

"Yes," I replied.

I couldn't bring myself to say anything else, but luckily Dawn jumped into the conversation. "We've noticed a pattern," she said. "People get married, then they have babies. Or they adopt babies or children."

"Not everyone," said Sharon. "Besides, between Richard and me we already have three children. And a cat."

"But don't the two of you want to have a baby together?" I asked.

"No," Sharon answered gently. "Not at this point in our lives."

"We're happy just the way we are," added Dad.

His voice carried that final note, the one that means, "End of discussion." The one that means, "I don't want to hear another word about it."

38

Dawn got the message, too. "Dinner's almost ready," she said.

So we ate dinner. No one said anything further about babies. But I couldn't stop *thinking* about them. Especially what to name a baby. I doodled in the margin of my maths homework that evening: Tara, Lizzie, Margaret, Tara, Adele, Tara, Frannie, Tara, Charity, Bea . . .

5th CHAPTER

When Logan and I had worked out our finances for Modern Living class, we'd drawn some pretty negative conclusions: flat rents were much higher than we'd expected; food was expensive; everything was expensive. And we could not yet be financially independent.

"What are we supposed to say in the lesson tomorrow?" Logan asked. "Somehow, I have the feeling that 'we can't afford anything' isn't what Mrs Boyden wants to hear. We could have told her that without doing *any* homework."

So Logan and I had written a two-page paper outlining how much money we earn, comparing the rents of different-sized flats, and trying to work out what percentage of someone's salary should be spent on rent alone, and therefore how much we would need to earn to afford even the tiniest little flat. We made four professional-looking graphs, too. (We used Magic Markers, coloured dots, rulers, even a protractor.)

Guess what. The day those homework assignments were due, we never even discussed them. We walked into our Modern Living classroom to find Mrs Boyden sitting at her desk, her hands clasped in front of her. On the desk was a carton of eggs, the lid open. Mrs Boyden said nothing as we filed into the room.

Something was going to happen.

"Logan," I dared to whisper, "do you think Mrs Boyden is angry with our class? Have we done something wrong?"

Logan shrugged. "Beats me."

To be on the safe side, I handed in our homework assignment. I laid it silently on the edge of our teacher's desk. The other kids watched, then did the same thing.

When we were all sitting quietly, Mrs Boyden got to her feet. She smiled. "Congratulations," she said. "You have all become parents."

"Huh?" said Shawna.

"You've been married for a while," Mrs Boyden continued, "and now you have had babies. Congratulations."

I noticed a lot of confused faces in the room.

Mrs Boyden indicated the carton of eggs.

"Your children," she said. "When I call your names, please come to the front of the room and receive your egg. Logan Bruno and Mary Anne Spier."

Feeling both confused and self-conscious, Logan and I made our way to Mrs Boyden's desk. She held out an egg, which Logan accepted (because my hand was sort of shaking). When she didn't say anything else, we returned to our seats.

Pair by pair, the other kids were given eggs also. While Logan waited for everyone to sit down, he played with our egg. He placed it in the middle of his desk, tapped it, sent it rolling, then caught it just before it sailed over the edge.

"Each of you now has a child," Mrs Boyden announced, closing the lid on the carton. "The eggs are your children. For the next few weeks you are to treat the eggs as you would infants."

At that moment, Logan had just rolled our egg to the edge of his desk again. He caught it in a hurry. He handed it to me.

"Your babies," Mrs Boyden was saying, "must be fed regularly, clothed, taken to the doctor, and especially, watched over. Just as you would never leave a human baby alone, you must never leave your egg alone. Someone must be available to care of it at all times. You will be in charge of your egg-babies for a month. At the end of four weeks, a paper will be due. I will expect you to write about your experiences, any problems you encountered, the solutions to those problems, and so forth. We'll talk more about the papers later this week. By the way, as parents you are responsible for your children, starting immediately. Of course, I won't be able to see that your babies are cared for when you're out of school, so everyone is on his or her honour this month. Every eighth-grader will become a parent to an egg, and I trust you to keep an eye on each other. Only you can make the honour system work.

Now, any questions?" our teacher asked.

As you can imagine, nearly everybody raised a hand.

"Shawna?" said Mrs Boyden.

"Do we really have to take our eggs to the doctor?" she asked. "I might feel sort of silly. I mean, what will the doctor think?"

Mrs Boyden closed her eyes momentarily. "No, you don't actually have to take your egg to a doctor. But you are going to be a mother for a month, so I expect you to know when and why your child might need to see a doctor. Remember to plan for check-ups."

Logan nudged me. "How are we supposed to feed these eggs?" he asked.

I shrugged.

Shawna put up her hand again and spoke without waiting to be called on. "About food—" she began to say.

"No, you do not need to prepare food and pretend to feed your egg," Mrs Boyden broke in. "Let me explain the project in more detail. When you leave this room at the end of the period, either you or your partner—your spouse—must watch over your child every moment. You wouldn't leave an infant unattended, so do not leave your egg in your locker during school hours. The egg will accompany you to classes. You must also tend to your egg after school and at night."

"Hey, what about after-school sports?" exclaimed a boy in the front row. "I can't watch an egg while I'm at baseball practice."

"Ask your wife to watch your child, then," said Mrs Boyden.

"But I take piano lessons," spoke up the wife. She hesitated, then added, "I suppose I could take the egg along with me."

Mrs Boyden nodded. "That would be an acceptable solution, as long as you keep your eye on the baby throughout the lesson."

Mrs Boyden mentioned some facts about babies. Not everyone was aware, for example, that small babies cannot hold their own bottles. "What does that tell you about feeding your baby?" asked Mrs Boyden.

"I suppose we have to be *with* our egg at mealtimes," spoke up Trevor Sandbourne. "The baby can't eat by itself."

"Right. In fact, you need to *hold* the egg," pointed out Mrs Boyden. "Small babies can't sit up, either. Understand?" We nodded. "One last thing," our teacher went on, glancing at the clock. "From now on, I would like you to refer to your children *as* children, rather than as eggs." Mrs Boyden didn't explain this—the bell rang just as she finished her sentence—so I didn't have a chance to ask her *why* we weren't supposed to call our eggs eggs.

Around me, my classmates were getting to their feet. But not Logan. He turned to me with this incredible, horrified expression on his face. Then he looked at our egg. I mean, our child. It was resting on my desk inside a little barricade I had created with my notebook, purse, and two textbooks. For the time being it was safe, but—

"We can't carry that, um . . . we can't carry *that* around all day," said Logan, pointing at our child.

"Just what I was thinking," I answered. "But we have to."

"Yeah. Okay. Where will it be safe? In my school bag?"

"Not the way you sling that thing around. I'll put our child in my bag. She'll be safe there."

"Are you sure she won't suffocate? And how do you know it's a girl?"

"I don't. I just want a girl. And she won't suffocate. My bag doesn't close, see?" (My bag was a big woven bag. It was great for school because I could throw lots of stuff into it, and I didn't have to worry about zipping or unzipping it all day.)

"Okay," said Logan uncertainly.

"Hey, come on, this is going to be fun," I told him. I was standing up, settling our daughter in my bag.

"But what about gym? You and I have gym at the same time now. What are we going to do with her then? I'll be playing baseball. I can't bring her out on the field with me. It's too hot. Anyhow, I'd probably sit on her."

"Don't panic," I said, although I felt a teensy bit panicky myself. "I'll be doing aerobics in my gym class. I'll bring my bag with me and leave it where I can see it. She'll be fine."

"All right. I suppose I'm just a nervous father."

"Well, relax. You're with kids all the time. You're great with them. Pretend you're babysitting or something."

Logan relaxed. He looked fondly at our child, now nestled in a wad of tissues in my bag. "Maybe we should name her," he suggested.

"Yes, but not now, dear. We're going to be late for our next class." I picked up my books and slipped my bag over my shoulder.

Logan peered worriedly inside the bag. "Take care of our child," he said. "Be particularly careful during gym. Why don't you give her to me at lunch and I'll watch her for the rest of the day?"

"Oh, no," I said. "You are not putting our daughter in your schoolbag. This afternoon we'll get together and work out a way to carry her around. I don't mind watching her today."

I had thought I might feel silly worrying about our child all day. I mean, how was I supposed to explain to my gym teacher that I needed to keep my bag nearby during aerobics so that I could babysit for an egg? But of course I wasn't the only pupil with that problem. A lot of other girls who had also attended their Modern Living classes earlier that day were in the same situation. And I saw a couple of them just put their eggs on the floor and leave them. How would they be able to tell them apart at the end of the lesson?

"Logan!" I exclaimed, when I met him in the cafeteria at lunchtime. "We have to label our baby or something. What if she got lost? We wouldn't be able to tell her from any other egg. I mean, baby."

"This afternoon we'll paint her with food colouring," said Logan. "It's painless *and* non-toxic. You have to think of those things."

I nodded. "Listen, I'm sure she's hungry by now. Why don't you eat while I feed her? Then I'll eat while you finish feeding her. We should probably feed her again at . . ."

6th CHAPTER

Tuesday

When I accepted the job with the Papadakis kids, I expected to babysit for just three children— Linny, Hannie, and Sari. I mean, the Papadakises only have three children. But I ended up bringing a fourth with me. My new son, Izzy the egg. My husband, Alan Gray, wanted to watch Izzy after school, but he wouldn't have been able to watch him in the evening, so I just brought Izzy home with me that afternoon, and at 3:45, carried him across the street to the Papadakises'. I think Izzy kind of confused the kids, but what would you expect?

49

Well, of all things. Alan Gray has been Kristy's enemy (okay, her pest) for as long as I can remember. And who does she end up marrying in her Modern Living class? Alan. How unfair.

How unfortunate. Kristy had a cow.

But that was on the day they got married. On the day they became parents, Kristy changed her mind about Alan. He turned out to be a pretty good father. First of all, he named Izzy.

"A son called Izzy," he had said dreamily to Kristy as he'd held his child for the first time.

"Izzy?" repeated Kristy. "What kind of name is that? Especially for a boy. I've never heard of a boy called Izzy."

"It's short for, um . . ."

"It's short for Isabelle or Isadora or Elizabeth," said Kristy.

"Oh, it must be short for some boy's name," said Alan offhandedly. "Anyway, don't you think it's a nice name?"

"It *is* sort of cute," Kristy had agreed, pleased that Alan was at least taking an interest in the project.

By Tuesday, the day of Kristy's job at the Papadakises', both she and Alan were taking more than a little interest in Izzy. They had made this elaborate "environment" for him in a shoe box. The box was lined with pieces of flannel so Izzy would always be comfortable. The sides of the box were covered with felt so Izzy wouldn't hurt himself if he bumped into a wall. Alan had placed a tiny music box in the environment so Izzy would feel comforted and develop an appreciation for music. And Kristy had stuck tiny charts and pictures on the felt so Izzy's learning cells would be stimulated. She claimed she read aloud to him at night, but I don't know.

Also, unlike a lot of the couples in Modern Living, Kristy and Alan fought over who got to take their child home after school (as opposed to who got *stuck* with him after school). They were conscientious parents. Which is why Kristy never even considered leaving Izzy at her house while she went to the Papadakises'. Of *course* he went along with her.

The Papadakis kids are good friends of Kristy's younger brothers and sisters. Linny, who's nine, plays with David Michael. Hannie, who's seven, is one of Karen's two best friends. And Sari, the little one, sometimes plays with Emily. Kristy and the kids are pals. So Kristy decided that her first order of babysitting business should be to explain Izzy to them.

As Mrs Papadakis backed down the drive, Kristy sat at the kitchen table with Linny and Hannie. Sari, who had just woken up from a nap, was sitting sleepily in her high chair.

Kristy placed Izzy's environment on the table. She pointed to her son. "This," she said, "is Izzy Thomas-Gray."

"That egg?" replied Linny, after a moment's hesitation.

"Well, yes," answered Kristy. "Only he isn't—"

"*He*?" interrupted Linny.

"—he isn't just an egg," Kristy continued. "He's my son."

"You mean your pre*tend* son . . . don't you?" asked Hannie. She peered into the shoe box and stared at Izzy.

"Well, yes. My pretend son," Kristy agreed. Then she tried to explain Mrs Boyden's Modern Living project to the kids.

"Okay, so you're pretend-married," said Linny, "and this egg is your pretend son. And you're babysitting for him, as well. Right?"

"Right."

"Where is Izzy's food?" asked Hannie.

"The food is pretend, too," Kristy answered. "I just have to spend time with Izzy as *if* I were feeding him. A bit like when you play with your dolls. You don't give them real food. Only with Izzy I have to remember to feed him every day, as often as—"

Ring, ring!

Linny bounded to his feet and made a grab for the phone. "I'll get it!" he cried. He picked up the receiver and said politely, "Hello, Papadakises' residence. Who's calling, please? . . . For Kristy? . . . Okay." Linny held the phone towards Kristy. "For you. I think it's your pretend husband."

"Hello?" said Kristy. "Alan? What's up?"

"I'm just checking on Izzy," he replied. "I was sitting here thinking about him, and . . . Is everything okay?"

"Oh, yes. Fine. Izzy's napping."

"Napping? Shouldn't he be eating? I don't think he eats enough. We don't want him to get scrawny."

"Alan, trust me. He's fine," said Kristy. "Um, except for—"

"WHAT?" exclaimed Alan. "Except for what?"

"He seems kind of nervous here."

"I thought he was asleep."

"He is now. But when we first got to the Papadakises', he was really shy."

"Well, you know, new faces."

"Yeah, but I'm concerned that he's not socializing properly."

Kristy and Alan discussed Izzy's social development. They talked for quite a while. They talked for so long that the kids

53

became bored, and Linny lifted Sari out of her high chair, nudged Kristy, and whipered loudly, "We're going to the playroom."

"Okay," Kristy answered distractedly. Ten minutes later, she finished her conversation with Alan, hung up the phone, and headed for the kids' playroom. Halfway there she realized she was without Izzy, and she dashed back to the kitchen. The table was empty. Had Izzy been in the kitchen when Kristy finished her phone conversation? She couldn't remember. She glanced round the room, decided he wasn't in it, and headed for the playroom again, calling, "Linny? Hannie?"

"Yeah?" Linny called back.

"Have you got Izzy?"

"Huh?"

"I said, 'Have you got Izzy?'" By then, Kristy had reached the playroom. The first thing she saw was Izzy's environment. The box was on Hannie's small colouring table. "Never mind," said Kristy. She ran for the box.

It was empty.

I mean, it was empty of Izzy. Everything else was there—the flannel, the cell-stimulating pictures, the music box. Only Izzy was missing.

"Where is he? Where's Izzy?" cried Kristy with a gasp.

54

"Hey, funny!" exclaimed Linny. "Good joke. Get it? Where *is* he? Where's *Izzy*?" He laughed loudly.

Hannie began to laugh, too. "Where Izzy? Where Izzy?" she sang.

Even Sari laughed and joined in.

"This isn't funny, you lot," said Kristy, her heart pounding. "Izzy is my baby. Remember? I'm responsible for him. Who brought this box in here? Linny?"

Linny's smile had faded. "Yeah, I did," he answered. "You were busy talking on the phone, and I thought Izzy might want to see the playroom."

"Okay." Kristy tried to calm down. "You brought this box in here? Then what? Did you take Izzy out of it?"

"Very, very gently," Hannie answered for her brother. Then she added, "*Very* gently. Honestly. Cross my heart."

"I believe you," said Kristy. "Just tell me where you put Izzy."

Hannie frowned. She looked at Linny, who was frowning, too. "Linny was holding onto Izzy tightly and he walked—"

"How tightly?" Kristy interrupted.

"Not *that* tightly," said Linny.

"Linny showed Izzy around the playroom," Hannie continued. "He showed him the bookshelf and Sari's rocking horse and the art cupboard and the trucks and cars, and then . . ."

"Yeah?" prompted Kristy.

"I think he stopped to look at his collection of bottle caps."

"Oh, that's right," agreed Linny. "So I put Izzy on the floor and, um, that's all I remember. Until you came in."

"Everybody, spread out and search!" yelped Kristy.

"Hmm. If I were an egg, where would I go?" muttered Linny.

"How about the fridge?" suggested Hannie.

She and Linny got the giggles. While Kristy tossed aside books and toys and sweaters, looking for her missing son, Hannie and Linny cracked jokes and laughed helplessly.

"Maybe Izzy is off looking for Humpty Dumpty," said Hannie.

"Egg-sactly!" cried Linny. "Or maybe he had a great fall."

"Egg-cellent," said Hannie.

"I hope nobody found Izzy and then . . . cooked him and ate him," added Linny. "That would set a bad egg-zample."

By that time, Kristy was no longer listening to Hannie and Linny. "Come on, Sari. You'll help me, won't— Hey, Sari, what are you doing?" Kristy knelt beside Sari, who was squatting on the floor. At her feet was a doll's blanket. Sari was patting it and saying, "Baby, baby."

Kristy poked the blanket. Then she

pulled at it. Inside was Izzy. "Oh, thank heaven! You're safe!" cried Kristy. "It's okay, Linny, Hannie. I found him. Guess what. Sari was taking care of Izzy for us."

"Drat. No more egg-citement," said Linny.

Even Kristy couldn't help laughing. "Linny!" she exclaimed.

"Sorry," he said. "It's just . . . I don't know. Your *son*? An egg named Izzy? I never heard of anything like that."

"Egg-straordinary, isn't it?" said Kristy. And then she replaced Izzy in his safe environment.

She decided not to tell Alan what had happened.

7th CHAPTER

Our daughter had a name. She went without one for four days while Logan and I argued over what to call her. I was holding out for Tara, but Logan didn't like the name. He wanted to call her Sally, which I thought was much too plain. Finally we compromised.

We named our child Samantha.

I thought Samantha was almost as beautiful as Tara, and that Sammie was an adorable nickname. Logan liked Sammie, too, because it sounded like Sally.

We lined a wicker basket for Sammie with scraps of pink fabric. The day we had been given Sammie, we had painted pink flowers on her with food colouring. The day we named her, we added this:

S"Now we'll always be able to recognize her," said Logan.

"*And* she's beautiful," I added. "Our beautiful daughter."

As soon as Sammie's basket was ready, Logan took on more than his share of the work in caring for our daughter. He took her home with him almost every afternoon. He carried her around school as often as possible.

He was a natural father.

Of course, he couldn't care for Sammie *all* the time, though. And one morning he met me at school, basket in hand, and said, "Just as I was leaving the house, Hunter reminded me that I promised to take him and Kerry to the playground this afternoon. I'm worried about taking Sammie with me. I don't want her to get too much sun."

"I'll take her," I said. "I'm babysitting for Rose and Ricky after school, but that shouldn't be a problem. It'll probably be easier for me to look after three babies than for you to take care of one baby and two active kids. I mean, the twins can't walk yet.

How much harder could three babies be than two?"

I found out at the Salems' house. Three could be plenty harder than two, and even two could be . . . a nightmare.

The bad dream began shortly after Mrs Salem left the house, when Ricky woke up from his nap.

He woke up crying.

I had been sitting in the kitchen with Sammie's basket in my lap (while supposedly I gave Sammie a bottle), when I heard snuffles and tears from the twins' bedroom.

"I'm coming!" I called gently, so as not to wake the other twin.

I stood up. "Sorry, Sammie," I said. "You'll have to finish your bottle later." I knew that wasn't quite fair. If Sammie had been a real baby, I would have had to work out how to feed her *and* rush upstairs. As it was, I had to bring her with me.

I entered the babies' room and found a very unhappy Ricky. He was sitting at one end of the cot, wailing, tears streaming down his face.

"Shh, Ricky, shh," I whispered. "What's the matter?"

I put Sammie on the changing table and picked up Ricky. I rocked him and walked him around the room until I realized that Rose was stirring. Then I took him into the hallway—and realized I'd left Sammie behind. A small baby should never be left on a changing table unattended. So I went back to retrieve her, and Ricky's cries woke Rose, who also began to cry.

"Hey, come on, you two. I can't hold both of you," I said, remembering at the same time that I hadn't finished feeding Sammie. Then the thought occurred to me that the twins were probably hungry. Also, that they could hold their own bottles. So I settled the babies in their high chairs and handed each one a bottle. Perfect. They could feed themselves while I fed Sammie.

Well, that worked in theory. In reality, Rose continued to fuss, so I held Sammie in my lap and fed Rose myself. This arrangement lasted until Ricky threw his bottle on the floor.

I stopped what I was doing, picked it up, handed it to him, and went back to Rose. Ricky threw down the bottle again. I decided Sammie had eaten enough and stood between the twins, holding Rose's bottle with my right hand and Ricky's with my left.

When the bottles were empty, I stepped back and examined the babies.

"You two look simply delightful," I told them. (I didn't mean it.)

They were far from the beautiful babies I'd dressed on my last sitting job. They were wearing crumpled T-shirts and damp nappies. Their cheeks were tearstained and their chins were milk-covered.

"Time to clean you up," I said decisively.

With difficulty, I returned Sammie, Rose, and Ricky to the twins' room. I put Rose in her cot, Sammie on the windowsill, and Ricky on the changing table. I removed Ricky's wet nappy.

"Wah!" he wailed.

He cried the *entire* time I changed him.

"You aren't getting ill, are you?" I asked. I felt his forehead. No temperature. And his appetite had seemed fine. When he was dry and powdered, I returned him to his cot and placed Rose on the table. She cried noisily while I changed her.

"Having a bad day?" I said to the twins.

They stared at me from tear-filled eyes.

At least their bottoms were dry.

"How about a walk?" I suggested. Walks are good for stopping tears.

I removed two lovely outfits from the wardrobe. For Rose, a white ruffled dress with matching knickerbockers and a hat, and her pink shoes. For Ricky, a frog jumpsuit with a matching shirt and hat, and his tiny high-topped trainers.

The babies eyed all those clothes warily. They turned on the tears before I'd even so much as lifted Ricky's arms. In the end, they left the house wearing fresh clothes, and socks. No earrings or frills for Rose. No hat for either of them. Not even shoes. At least they'd whittled down their crying to sniffles and hiccups. They weren't happy, but they were quiet.

I hung Sammie's basket over a handle of the double buggy. Then I set out with the three babies. For a while, they were quiet. They seemed content. I managed to convince myself that Sammie had had enough to eat and I hadn't neglected her *too* badly. I relaxed.

And Rose began bumping back and forth in her seat and making these awful whiny noises. She wasn't exactly crying, but—

Time for distraction technique. "What a beautiful day!" I exclaimed. I pointed to the sky. "Look, I see a bird. Bird."

"Ba!" said Rose.

"That's right. Bird. And there's a cloud."

We stopped next to a garden. "Ooh, pretty flowers," I said.

Ricky reached for a tulip, got a grip on the stem, and pulled.

The plant uprooted, sending dirt flying.

"Ricky!" I cried. I whirled round and looked at the house beyond the garden. What if someone had seen us? "Ricky!" I said again. "No, no, no!" I took the flower from him and dropped it in the garden. I

tried to bury it under some leaves. Then for
good measure, I said "No!" to Ricky once
more.

Both babies, looking bewildered, burst
into tears.

Uh-oh. "Sorry, Ricky. I'm sorry," I said.
"Rose, I'm sorry. I didn't mean to shout.
But Ricky, you can't go around pulling up
plants. That flower isn't yours. It belongs to
someone else." (As if he could really
understand me.)

I wheeled the buggy away quickly and
hurried down the pavement with my cargo
of crying babies. If Logan had been at
home, I *might* have phoned him and asked
him to come and get Sammie. But I coped as
well as I could.

"That was a nightmare, all right," Dawn
said that evening, when I described my job
at the Salems' to her.

"Yeah. I suppose it could have been
worse though."

"How? If the house had burned down?"

"No, if, um, well, I'm not sure. I mean,
this just wasn't realistic, that's all. I don't
usually babysit for three babies at once.
I have to admit, I thought the job wouldn't
be too bad since the babies can't walk. I
should have realized how silly that is. I still
have only one pair of hands, and most
people take care of just one baby at a time.
Anyway, nothing bad actually happened

this afternoon. The babies were fussy, but you have to expect that. I still want a little sister, don't you? A real one, I mean. Not an egg one. Even a little brother would be okay."

"Yeah, I still want a sister or brother," Dawn replied. "And you know what came in the post today?"

"What?"

"The Kumbel catalogue."

"The *Kum*bel catalogue?" I shrieked. The Kumbel catalogue sells *every*thing. Dawn knows what my favourite section is. Baby supplies and furnishings. "Where is it?"

"In my room. I'll go and get it." Dawn dashed across the landing, then returned to my bedroom, clutching the fat catalogue.

I found the baby section in about three seconds. "Ah, look!" I exclaimed. "Look at that cot. It would be perfect for a girl *or* a boy. White with yellow stars and a moon."

"It *is* adorable," agreed Dawn. "And we could get that matching chest of drawers and rocking chair. A yellow-and-white baby's room would be so cute."

"If Dad and Sharon had a baby," I said thoughtfully, "I suppose you and I would end up sharing a room again." (We had tried that once. It hadn't worked.) "My room would become the baby's room."

"No, the baby could have Jeff's room, I think."

"Oh, whatever. Hey, look at *that*! A baby's lamp with a stars-and-moon shade. Tara would *have* to have that."

"Tara?" said three voices.

Drat. Dad and Sharon had overheard us talking again.

"Yeah. Our . . . baby sister?" I ventured.

"No," said Dad.

"No way," said Sharon.

"Double drat," I replied.

8th CHAPTER

Ten people attended the next meeting of the Babysitters Club. Seven humans and three small babies. (Okay, three eggs.) Sammie, Izzy, and Bobby.

Bobby was Stacey's little boy. (Claudia's child was over at his father's house.) He lived in a plastic mixing bowl. His father was Austin Bentley, a friend of Stacey's and Claudia's. Austin sometimes invites one or the other of them to school dances or to parties, but he isn't their boyfriend. (A good thing, too, because I think he'd have trouble choosing between them.) The three of them are just good friends.

Claud had fixed a sort of nursery in her room. The nursery was an area on her dressing table on which sat Sammie in her basket, Izzy in his shoe box environment, and Bobby in his mixing bowl. She had placed pillows on the floor around the dresser in case one of the babies fell off.

"Why don't you just put the babies on the floor?" asked Mal practically. "Then they wouldn't be able to fall."

"Too draughty," Kristy answered.

"So how are your kids getting on?" Jessi inquired politely.

"Sammie's fine," I said, "but Logan—"

"Order! Come to order, please!" said Kristy.

(I checked the official club time keeper. Sure enough. Five-thirty.)

My friends and I straightened up. We adjusted ourselves.

"Any club business?" our chairman wanted to know.

No one answered her. So I said simply, "Logan is hogging Sammie. Lately, he is almost always looking after her." Tears welled up in my eyes. "This is the first time I've brought her home after school since the day I babysat for the Tragedy Twins."

Stacey giggled. "You mean Ricky and Rose?"

"Yeah." I couldn't even laugh at my own joke.

The phone rang and Claud picked it up. "Hello, Babysitters Club. . . . Mm-hmm, mm-hmm. . . . In Karen Brewer's class? . . . Oh. . . . Thursday afternoon? I'll check and call you straight back." Claud hung up and said, "That was someone called Mr Gianelli. He said his son is in Karen's class at Stoneybrook Academy."

"Gianelli," repeated Kristy. "He must be Bobby's father."

"Right," said Claud. "The Gianellis have two kids, Bobby and his little sister, Alicia. They need a sitter on Thursday afternoon."

I looked at the appointment pages in the record book. "You can do it, Stace," I said. "Want the job?"

"Okay."

Claud phoned Mr Gianelli back while I scribbled in the BSC record book. I love filling in those blank pages.

"I don't know why you want to spend so much time with an egg," Stacey said to me. She brushed her hair out of her eyes.

I gasped. "Sammie is my *daugh*ter!" I exclaimed.

Stacey made a face. "Honestly, Mary Anne."

"You heard what Mrs Boyden said."

"Yeah, yeah. And I'm doing the project. So's Austin. We're very fair and careful. We each take care of Bobby exactly half the time. One day I bring him home, one day Austin brings him home. But what a pain. I don't think I have time for Modern Living class. Always having to stop and think about feeding Bobby or giving him a bath or something. On Monday I took him shopping with Mum and me. I thought a baby would need new vests and nappies and things pretty often. So I lugged the mixing bowl round four baby departments while Mum shopped for fun things, like books and presents. All I saw were baby thermometers and baby minders and baby trainers and baby toys and baby bottles and baby blankets. Babies certainly need a lot of equipment. I never even had a chance to look at clothes for *me*."

"Oh, but buying baby things is fun," I spoke up. I was thinking about the Kumbel catalogue.

"For five minutes," said Stacey.

"Well, anyway, I—I—" (I was trying to think of a nice way to say I didn't agree with Stacey.) "I suppose I don't mind shopping for baby things. And I *still* wish Logan wouldn't hog Sammie."

From her place on the floor, Mal tried to hide a giggle.

"What's so funny?" asked Dawn.

"Mary Anne keeps saying Logan is *hogging* Sammie. And 'hogging' makes me think of bacon. And Sammie is an egg. Get it? Bacon and eggs?" Mallory snorted with laughter.

Jessi began to laugh, too.

But us five older club members remained serious. After a few moments, Claud said, "You two don't understand. You aren't parents yet."

Mal and Jessi calmed down.

We took a few phone calls. Then Kristy got up from the director's chair, crossed the room to the dresser, and peeped into Izzy's box. "I think Izzy is getting spoiled," she said.

"Too much attention?" I asked.

"No, I mean I think he's spoiling. Smell him."

Kristy is forever asking me to smell disgusting things. I don't know why she thinks I'll do it.

"No, thanks," I replied.

But brave Dawn stood up and sniffed around in the box. "I can't smell anything," she said. "You're making up worries."

"I am not," Kristy replied. However, she sat down again.

"You lot, what's being married like?" asked Jessi.

"Yeah, what's it like?" echoed Mal.

"Well," Stacey began after a moment, "I don't know what to compare it to. But a lot of it is communicating. With your husband or wife. You have to be able to talk about who's going to watch the baby when, and who has to remember to do which things with the baby."

"And you have to agree on things," added Kristy. "And trust your husband. That's really important. You have to trust him."

"Being married is expensive," I added.

"Nobody has said anything about love," pointed out Jessi.

The room grew silent.

"Yeah, aren't you supposed to be in love?" asked Mal.

"I suppose that *would* make things easier," said Stacey slowly. "If I were actually in love with Austin, I'd want to spend more time with him. And I'd want our child to spend more time with us. Maybe being married wouldn't seem like *quite* so much work."

"I know what you mean," I said. "Marriage would still be difficult and expensive. But, boy, if I didn't love Logan—Um, if I didn't *like* him a lot—" (I was blushing.)

Dawn smiled. "You can say 'love,' Mary Anne."

"Okay. If I didn't love him, I could never be married to him and take care of Sammie with him. It's hard enough when we do love each other. . . . Oh, I almost forgot. I have to feed—"

The phone rang. Jessi picked it up. "Logan? Okay, hang on a sec." Jessi handed the phone to me. "It's your husband."

"Hi, dear," I said.

"Hi. Did you feed Sammie?"

"I was just about to."

"Okay. By the way, is Claudia's room warm enough?"

"Yes." Logan reminded me of Kristy and Alan.

"Maybe you should add a little blanket to the basket."

"But it's almost seventy degrees outside . . . *dear*," I said. "Sammie is fine. Or she will be after I feed her."

Logan let me hang up and feed Sammie. Kristy fed Izzy, and Stacey fed Bobby. "You know," said Kristy, "if we really had to feed babies, we'd have to stop and prepare their feeds. That would take even more time. I think we're getting off easy."

"I *still* wish Logan would let me look after Sammie more often," I said. "Sometimes I think he doesn't trust me."

"Oh, he's just being overprotective," said Claud.

There seemed to be a lot of that going around.

"Well, I think you should all just feel lucky that you *don't* actually have babies," said Jessi. "That this is just a school project."

"And that it will be over in less than a month," added Mal. "I remember when my mum was pregnant with Claire. If she had been at school then, she would have had to drop out."

"Mallory. She had six *other* kids to look after," said Kristy.

"That's not what I mean. You don't know how tired you feel when you're pregnant. And you're even tireder after the baby comes. Busier, too."

Hmm. I wondered if Sharon could handle her job, as well as being "tireder" and busier than usual. Well, of course she could. Dawn and I would help her whenever she wanted. She would only have to do one third of the usual mothering. Now, if she and Dad would just come to their senses.

9th
CHAPTER

Thursday

who knew an egg could be so scary?
Well, maybe I should have known.
when I was five I went through
this phase during which I was
terrified of pigeons for no good
reason. Anyway, I sat for Bobby
and Alicia Gianelli this afternoon,
and Alicia... well, when she first
saw my son she screamed. Mrs
Gianelli hadn't said anything
about Alicia having an egg phobia,
so I suppose it was the surprise
of finding an egg underneath the
flannels in the mixing bowl.
Maybe she expected a kitten or
something. Also, the egg's name
was the same as her brother's.
I suppose that was confusing.

The Gianellis were new clients of the BSC. None of us had babysat for them before the afternoon of Stacey's job. Kristy knew Bobby slightly because he's in Karen's class at school. That was how the Gianellis had heard about the BSC. But basically they were uncharted territory. You know, a new experience.

Uncharted territories and new experiences make me nervous, but Stacey enjoys a good challenge. She was looking forward to her job at the Gianellis'. She adores meeting people, especially kids.

Stacey walked straight to the Gianellis' house after school. She ran up their front steps, stuck her finger out to ring the bell, and realized there was a piece of tape over it. (Over the bell, that is. Not over her finger.) To the left of the bell was a small sign that read, CHILD SLEEPING, PLEASE KNOCK.

Stacey knocked lightly on the door, and it was opened by this tall man with a moustache. "Hi, I'm Mr Gianelli," he whispered.

"I'm Stacey McGill," Stacey replied.

Mr Gianelli ushered Stace inside, quietly explaining that Mrs Gianelli was at work, Alicia was napping, and Bobby had not yet come home from school. "He takes the bus," said Mr Gianelli in explanation. Then he noticed Stacey's mixing bowl. "What's that?" he asked.

Stacey began to tell him about Mrs Boyden and Modern Living, but Mr Gianelli interrupted her. "Ah, the egg project," he said. "I know it well. I used to be a teacher. Good luck."

He gave Stacey some instructions, showed her where important things (like the first-aid kit) were kept, handed her a list of emergency phone numbers, then left to go to a meeting in Stamford.

Stacey sat at the kitchen table and waited for Bobby to come home or for Alicia to wake up. While she waited, she talked to her own Bobby, the one in the plastic mixing bowl.

"Pretend I'm feeding you," she said wearily to the egg. "By the way, you're going over to your father's house tonight instead of tomorrow. I can't take care of you tonight. I'm way behind in everything, thanks to—"

"Are you the babysitter?" asked a sleepy voice.

Stacey whirled her head round. She hadn't heard anyone come into the kitchen. Standing a few metres away, apparently keeping her distance, was a dark-haired, dark-eyed little girl with olive skin. She looked curiously from Stacey to the mixing bowl and back to Stacey.

"Hi!" Stacey said brightly. "Yes, I'm your sitter. My name is Stacey. Stacey McGill. You must be Alicia."

The girl nodded. Then she held up four fingers. "I'm this many," she added.

"I bet you've just had your birthday."

Alicia nodded again. "What's in the bowl?" she asked. "What are you talking to?" She stepped closer to Stacey.

Stacey grinned. "I think you'll be surprised. Want to see?"

"Okay." Alicia peered into the bowl.

Stacey pulled back the flannels. There was Bobby.

"Aaghhh!" shrieked Alicia. She burst into tears.

"What's the matter?" exclaimed Stacey.

"I don't like that thing! Why do you have it with you?"

Stacey paused, trying to work out what to tell Alicia. Before she had a chance to speak, the front door opened, then closed. "Bobby!" cried Alicia.

Bobby Gianelli hurtled into the kitchen and flung his school bag on the floor. "I'm home!" he announced. "Hi, Alicia. Hi, babysitter."

Alicia was still crying. "Bobby, look in that bowl," she said, pointing.

Bobby took a look at Bobby. "Weird," he said. He opened the fridge and removed a carton of milk. "Whose is it?"

"It's mine," Stacey answered. And then she explained about the Modern Living project. "And you'll never guess what," she said finally.

"What?" asked Bobby. He and Alicia were sitting at the table, facing Stacey. They looked at her seriously.

"His name is Bobby."

"That *egg's* name is Bobby?" said Bobby.

Stacey nodded. "Well, remember, I'm supposed to pretend it's my baby, not just an egg. And if he were my baby, I would have named him."

"Right," said Bobby. He put his empty glass in the sink.

"So, Bobby, what do you want to do today?" asked Stacey.

Bobby opened a cupboard and looked inside. He closed the cupboard. Then he knelt down and opened his school bag.

"Bobby?" said Stacey again. (No answer.) Bobby?"

"Are you talking to me?" asked Bobby. Stacey nodded. "Oh, sorry. I thought you were talking to your egg. What do I want to do today? I don't know. Play football, I suppose, if the other kids will play. I'd better change into my kit." Bobby left the kitchen. From halfway up the stairs to the second floor he called, "Can I bring Bobby with me?"

"You *are* Bobby!" replied Alicia.

"I think he means this Bobby," Stacey said, tapping the mixing bowl. "I'll see!" she called back. (She was thinking, No way.)

"Oh, good. Let Bobby take that egg," said Alicia, who was sitting as far from the bowl as possible, her eyebrows knitted.

"Don't you like Bobby?" asked Stacey.

"He's my brother!" replied Alicia.

"I mean the egg. Are you afraid of Bobby the egg?"

"Yes."

"Are you afraid of all eggs?"

"No."

"Then why are you afraid of Bobby?"

"I'm not. He's my—"

"Bobby the *egg!*"

"I never saw an egg in bed before."

"Pretend he's a baby, not an egg."

At that moment, Bobby the boy returned to the kitchen in his football kit, which turned out to be a sweatshirt, a pair of jeans, and a bicycle helmet. "Okay, I'm ready," he said. "Is the egg?"

"Is *Bobby*," Alicia corrected him.

"What?" said Bobby.

"What?" said Stacey.

"Never mind," said Alicia.

"I'm ready to play football with the egg," said Bobby.

Yikes, thought Stacey. "Bobby," she said, "*I* have to look after the egg. He belongs to me. Do you understand?"

"Sort of." Bobby left then, saying he would be over the road.

"Okay, Alicia, what do *you* want to do?" asked Stacey.

"Walk to the stream. But not with Bobby."

Stacey sighed. Then she saw that Alicia was truly frightened, so she called Austin Bentley and asked him to come and pick up Bobby early. Luckily, he was at home. Later, after he and Bobby left, Stacey and Alicia walked down the street to the little stream. Alicia sat on a sunny rock and tossed pebbles into the water. Stacey sat on a patch of dry grass and thought. What if Bobby had been her real child and she had no husband to call on for help? she wondered. What did you do if you were a single parent and you were at work and your child got ill and the nurse phoned and said he should come home from school? What if you couldn't leave your job? Or what if you were at home and something happened to you and you simply needed help?

"I bet my mum is scared sometimes," Stacey said over the phone to me that night. "I bet she wonders about the 'what ifs.' Like what if she got a job and she was at work and I was at school and I went into a diabetic coma? Or what if something happened to *Mum* and no one could get in touch with my dad? I bet Mum worries a lot, Mary Anne."

"I think all parents do," I replied.

"But they probably feel a little safer if they aren't *single* parents."

"Mm. Maybe. Stace? Are you worried because you're the daughter of a divorced mum? And your dad doesn't live nearby? That would be okay. I used to worry more when my dad was single."

"Yeah. I worry sometimes." Stacey paused. "You know, this afternoon was kind of funny with two Bobbies, and Alicia afraid of the egg and everything. But I decided something. I am going to wait until I'm *really old* before I have a human baby."

10th CHAPTER

Ever since we had our baby, Logan and I had spent very little time alone together. We hadn't been out—just the two of us—for ages. How many places can you easily take a baby to? I suppose we *could* have taken Sammie to Pizza Express or the diner or the coffee shop, but it just didn't seem like a great idea. Anyway, Logan and I would have been busy feeding Sammie, holding her, and doing all those things you have to do to occupy a baby, and that would have sort of defeated the purpose.

But one Friday, at the end of Modern Living class, Logan said to me, "Mary Anne, I'd really like us to go out tonight. I hate to leave Sammie behind, but . . . I don't know. I just want to go to the cinema or something."

Considering how attached Logan had become to our daughter, this seemed like an

83

especially nice idea. I think he was taking our class project a little more seriously than anyone, except maybe Alan and Kristy. If I hadn't known better, I might have thought he cared more about Sammie than he did about me. So a film sounded like a terrific idea, and I told him so. "Oh, Logan, great!" I exclaimed. "I can't wait. And don't worry about Sammie. I'll take care of everything."

"Great. I'll come to your house at six-thirty."

Ding-dong.

That evening, our doorbell rang promptly at six-thirty. Dad and Sharon were upstairs getting ready to go out to dinner. Dawn was babysitting for Haley and Matt Braddock.

I was standing at the front door holding Sammie in her basket.

When I let Logan inside, the first words out of his mouth were, "What's Sammie doing?" He took the basket from me.

"Sleeping?" I suggested.

"I mean, what's she doing *here*?"

"Coming with us," I answered. "We can't leave her alone."

"Didn't you get a babysitter?"

I shook my head. "Dad and Sharon are going out. Dawn's babysitting at the Braddocks'. I didn't want to ask any of them to look after Sammie."

"Well, what about someone else? Claudia or someone?"

"Oh, Logan. Can't we just bring Sammie with us? We don't have time to find a sitter now. We'll miss the beginning of the film."

"Bring a baby to the cinema? No way."

But in the end, that was what we did.

I checked Sammie to make sure the identifying marks on her shell still showed up. Then I added a large scrap of flannel to her basket, since our cinema starts using the air-conditioning around the middle of March, in order to keep the temperature at a pretty steady 45° all year-round.

"When's she due for her next feed?" Logan asked me, as we stood in the queue, that was stretching down the pavement.

"Right in the middle of the film," I answered. "But that'll be okay. One of us will be holding her anyway."

"Yeah. One of us will."

Something in Logan's tone of voice made me glance at him and wonder exactly how our evening was going to go. But just then the doors opened, and we filed inside along with the rest of the crowd. I got distracted juggling Sammie, my purse, and the extra sweaters I'd brought along. I forgot what Logan had said. And how he'd said it.

"Are you hungry?" Logan asked me, as we walked through the lobby.

"Sort of. Are you?"

"Starving. I didn't eat dinner. What do you want?"

"A small popcorn and a small diet Coke."

"Okay." Logan went up to the counter and said to the woman, "One small popcorn, one giant popcorn, one small diet Coke, one large diet Coke, and a large box of Peanut M&M's, please."

Well, not only did all that food cost a fortune, but the two of us couldn't carry it. Not with Sammie and the sweaters. We had to get one of those cardboard boxes like you get on trains, and then sort of hobble into the auditorium and down a darkened aisle.

"If we were really married and really on a budget," I said to Logan, as we looked for seats, "we could probably have paid our electricity bill with the money we spent on food and cinema tickets tonight."

"I know."

"Just think if we had to pay a babysitter, too."

"I suppose you have to splurge sometime," said Logan, but he looked as if he weren't sure he meant that.

The auditorium was getting crowded. Even so, I whispered to Logan, "I think we're going to need three seats tonight. We have so much stuff."

Luckily we found a row consisting of three empty seats. It was right over on the side of the auditorium and quite close to the front, but at least we'd found what we needed. I eased myself into the middle seat, and Logan sat on the aisle. I put Sammie in the third seat, the one by the wall. But she didn't weigh enough to hold the seat down.

It flipped back up, trapping Sammie and her basket between the seat and the seat back, "Yikes!" I cried.

Logan saw what had happened, but he was holding that flimsy box full of spilly drinks and popcorn. He needed both hands to carry it. Even so, he nearly dropped it. "Mary Anne!" he hissed.

"I'm *sorry*," I said crossly. I dropped my armload of sweaters and grabbed the handle of Sammie's basket with one hand and the seat with the other. I pushed the seat down and gingerly lifted the basket.

Sammie was safe inside.

"She's okay," I said to Logan.

"I knew this wasn't a good idea," he replied. "Okay. Now *hold* Sammie."

"I can't. I mean, I can't hold her *and* the popcorn *and* my drink. Just a sec." I pulled down the seat again and put the sweaters on it. "Do you want to give me your coat?" I asked Logan. (He actually likes the temperature in the auditorium.)

Logan put the tray of food on the floor, took off his coat, handed it to me, and picked up the food. Then I put Sammie on Logan's coat, and he handed me my popcorn and drink. At last we were settled.

"Excuse me, is that seat taken?"

Logan and I glanced up. Standing at Logan's elbow was a tall man in a suit. He was looking at Sammie's seat with raised eyebrows.

"Well," said Logan.

"Well," I said.

The man checked his watch. "The film is going to begin any minute now, and the auditorium is packed," he pointed out.

I thought about what might happen if I told the man the seat was occupied by an egg. The outcome didn't look good.

Logan must have been thinking the same thing, because he sighed and said, "No, it's not taken."

I gave Logan back his coat, which he sat on.

I put on one of the sweaters.

I sat on the others.

Then I put Sammie on my lap.

"Logan," I whispered as the lights began to dim, "I can't hold Sammie and eat, too." (My food was on the floor.)

"Neither can I," Logan replied. "Anyway I've got more food than you."

"All right. I'm going to put Sammie's basket on the floor until I've finished eating. She'll be okay there."

"Shhh!" hissed the man on the other side of me. He was the first person I've ever known who wanted to pay attention to the cartoon about not dropping litter in the auditorium, and buying fresh popcorn at the concession stand, and how to find the exits in case of fire.

"Sorry," I replied.

"You can't put Sammie on the floor!" Logan whispered loudly.

"SHHH!"

"Sorry."

I put Sammie on the floor anyway. "She's right between my feet," I said to Logan. "If anyone takes her basket, I'll know about it."

"Excuse me," said the man, "are you two going to talk through the *entire* film, or just this first part?"

"Sorry," I said again.

But Logan said, "I think just this first part." Only he said it so softly the man didn't hear him.

The film turned out to be really good. It was funny and exciting. I was glad of that. During the first half of the picture, Logan kept turning to me and grinning. He was relaxing. So was I.

Except for my right foot. It had gone

numb from being held in the same position for so long. Sammie or no Sammie, I had to shift my legs. So I did. Then I reached down to check on her. I felt around inside the basket.

Sammie had gone.

I gasped.

"What's the matter?" asked Logan.

"Sammie's not in the basket," I said. My heart was pounding. Logan grabbed up the basket. Then *he* felt around inside it. "She must have fallen out!" he exclaimed, trying to whisper. "You let her fall out. You lost our daughter!"

"I did not!"

"You did too. I bet she's rolling around in the aisle somewhere."

Logan was half right. Sammie was rolling around, but she wasn't in the aisle. She was just under my seat. Except we didn't discover that until after Logan had panicked and called over an usher to shine his torch on the floor. I thought the man in the third seat would kill us.

When Sammie was nestled safely in her basket again, Logan said stiffly, "Maybe we should hard-boil her." Then he tugged at my elbow. "Come on. We're going now, Mary Anne."

"Fine," I replied.

"Good," said the man.

Logan and I carried our stuff to the lobby, threw away our rubbish, and struggled into our coats. Logan picked up Sammie's basket.

"*I'm* supposed to have her tonight!" I cried.

"No way. You almost lost her," said Logan. "Not that I really want to take care of her *again*. I'm always taking care of her."

"You mean you're always *taking* her. You never let me have her."

"Okay, then *you* take her tonight."

"Oh, no. You don't trust me. You just said so."

Logan didn't answer. He grabbed Sammie's basket. Then he went off to call his parents for a lift home, and I called my dad, and Logan and I went off in a huff.

11th CHAPTER

Tuesday

Well, my brothers and sisters did it again.

I don't know why that surprises you anymore, Mal.

I don't know why, either. But really... it's a good thing my parents are so tolerant. They'll have to buy another dozen eggs tomorrow.

yeah. The kids were nice to skip, though. I think they liked him.

Lucky for him.

What's that supposed to mean?

Nothing. Never mind. Come on, Dawn, we're way off track. We'd better finish this notebook entry. We have a meeting tomorrow.

On Tuesday night Mr and Mrs Pike went to Parents' Evening at Stoneybrook Elementary School. Imagine what the evening is like for them. *Seven* of their kids are pupils at the school: Claire at nursery school, Margo in the second grade, Nicky in the third, Vanessa in the fourth, and the triplets in the fifth. No wonder they stay for the full three hours the school is open. (When I went to SES, my dad could do Parents' Evening in under an hour.)

While the Pikes visited SES, Mal and Dawn sat for Mal's younger brothers and sisters. Dawn left our house shortly after six-thirty. She left with her child, an egg named Skip. Skip lived in an empty Kleenex box, standard size. Dawn and her husband, this boy called Aaron Albright, whom Dawn didn't like very much, hadn't prepared the box except to line it with some paper towels to prevent Skip from injuring himself. (For the record, Dawn did *not* name Skip. Aaron did. Dawn said if she'd had her way, she would have named her son Douglas. She said Douglas is a good, strong name, and that Skip is what you'd name some little cartoon character, like maybe a young chicken wearing trainers and a cap.)

Dawn and Skip arrived at Mallory's just as Mr and Mrs Pike were getting ready to leave. Mal was trying to get the triplets to help her clear up the kitchen after dinner.

"Washing dishes is girls' work," Dawn heard Adam say.

"Adam," Mal replied, "there is no such thing as girls' work. But if there were, it would be called women's work."

"There *is* girls' work," said Adam.

"Is there boys' work?" Mal asked him.

"Of course."

"What is it?"

"Shovelling snow."

"I can do that," said Mal.

"Mowing lawns."

"I can do that, too."

"Cleaning gutters."

"And I can do that."

Adam turned away from his sister, looking pained. He couldn't win the argument, and he knew it. Luckily, when he turned round, he found a distraction. Dawn and the Kleenex box.

"Hi, everybody," said Dawn.

The youngest kids were still sitting at the kitchen table, dawdling over bowls of ice cream. Vanessa was sitting there, too, but a pad of paper lay in front of her. She was scribbling on it, probably composing a new poem. Mal was at the sink, and the triplets were hovering around the doorway, trying to escape the cleaning-up process.

Adam spotted Skip's box immediately. "What's that?" he asked.

"What's what?" answered Dawn, which only goes to show how accustomed my friends and I had grown to lugging around mixing bowls and Kleenex boxes and stuff.

"That box," said Adam.

"Yeah, what is it? It's too small to be a Kid-Kit," added Margo.

"Oh, it's Skip, my egg," said Dawn wearily. "I'm supposed to pretend he's my baby. You know, feed him and everything."

"Feed an *egg*?" asked Jordan.

"Well, not really. Dawn described the Modern Living experiment with a little help from Mallory.

The Pike kids were so interested that they hardly noticed when their parents left for the elementary school. "'Bye," they called vaguely.

"Dawn? How long will you be married to Aaron?" asked Vanessa.

"Hey, is your name Dawn Albright now?" Claire wanted to know.

"Yeah, do we have to call you Mrs Albright?" Nicky giggled.

"Oh, I hope not," said Dawn, but she was smiling. "Even if we had really, really, *really* got married, I wouldn't have changed my name. I like my name. I will always be Dawn Schafer."

Byron was looking into the tissue box

for about the ninety-fifth time. "Your baby is naked," he commented.

"Yeah, he isn't even wearing a nappy," chimed Vanessa.

"I wish I were married and had an egg-baby," said Margo.

"Me, too," said Vanessa. She looked hopefully at Byron.

Byron sighed. "Okay. I'll be your husband," he said. "But only for tonight."

"Who will be my husband?" asked Margo.

"Not me," said Adam defiantly. "I am never, *ever* getting married."

"Jordan?" said Margo.

"Oh, all right."

Surprisingly, Nicky agreed to be Claire's husband.

"Okay, let's adopt babies!" cried Vanessa.

"Adopt them from where?" asked Mal, even though she thought she knew what the answer would be.

"From the fridge, of course." Vanessa removed a half-empty carton of eggs from the bottom shelf of the fridge. She put it on the table and opened the lid carefully. "Ah, aren't they sweet?" she said.

"It's the egg nursery," added Nicky.

"Hey, there are enough here for each couple to adopt *two* children," Byron pointed out. "And Mum will still have one left over for tomorrow. Mal, can we? Adopt the eggs, I mean?"

"I suppose so," Mallory replied.

Several hands reached for the carton. They were stopped in midair by Jordan. "Wait! Where are you going to put them? We'd better prepare rooms or something for them."

"*My* children are not going to live in any tissue box," said Margo. "*My* children are going to live in a house. Come on, Jordan." Margo took two eggs and led her brother to the recreation room, where she succeeded in talking him into arranging up the doll's house for their children.

Meanwhile, Vanessa and Byron arranged their eggs in a shopping bag, and Claire and Nicky put theirs in eggcups.

"That's what eggcups are *for*," said Claire.

"And, now they're dressed," added Nicky. (Each eggcup was in the shape of a pair of crossed legs wearing blue trousers. On the feet were polka-dotted socks and big red clown shoes.)

"We'd better dress *our* babies," said Vanessa. "I don't want them to go around naked, like Skip."

"How are we going to dress them?" asked Byron. "I'm not sewing anything. I'll be these eggs' father, but not their tailor."

"Oh, we don't have time to sew clothes," Vanessa replied. "We'll just colour their outfits on with crayons." She fetched a box of crayons from a shelf in the recreation room. "Here we go." Vanessa aimed a yellow crayon at one egg. "A nice bright shirt for you. . . . Hey, this hardly shows up at all." Vanessa pressed down harder.

The egg broke.

"Oh! Oh, no! I've killed him!" shrieked Vanessa. "I've killed little—I've killed poor little, um, little—"

"We didn't even name him," said Byron sadly. "Poor egg."

"Poor, poor nameless killed egg," added Vanessa. She was holding the yellow crayon in one hand and the broken egg in the other. The yoke was sliming through her fingers and dripping onto the floor.

Dawn and Mallory both rushed forward—not to comfort Vanessa, but to cup their hands under the egg goo in an attempt to catch it.

"You stay here," Mal said to Dawn. "I'll go for the paper towels."

"The paper towels?!" wailed Vanessa. "Is that all you care about? The rug? Our egg has just been in a terrible accident. If *I* were in a terrible accident, would you run around trying to clean up my blood, or would you—"

"Vanessa! For heaven's sake, it's an *egg*," Mal reminded her.

"And you've only *known* the egg for a couple of minutes," said Dawn.

"I had grown attached," Vanessa replied stiffly.

Mal didn't answer. She ran off, then returned with a roll of paper towels and a plastic dustbin bag (bio degradable). While she and Dawn cleared up the mess, Vanessa watched sadly. She looked around the recreation room at Margo and Jordan, who were putting their eggs to bed in the doll's house, and at Nicky and Claire, who had loaded their eggs (in the cups) into a doll's buggy and were taking them for a walk to the garage door. Then she looked at Byron, who was lowering their remaining son into the paper bag.

"Mallory, may we please have that last egg?" she asked in a small voice.

"What—the one in the fridge?"

"Yes."

"Then we won't have *any* eggs." (Mallory had a sneaking suspicion that a few more accidents might occur.)

"But . . . but . . ." Vanessa's lower lip trembled. "My *baby*!"

"Maybe you should let her have it," Dawn whispered to Mal.

Mal sighed. "Okay. I don't think one egg is worth all this trouble." She turned to her sister. "Vanessa, you can have the egg."

"Oh, thank you! We'll be really careful this time, won't we, Byron? We won't try to dress either egg. They can be naked."

"Hey, you lot!" called Nicky. "We're taking our eggs out to dinner at a restaurant. Want to come with us?"

"Sure," agreed the other kids. And before long, the Pikes had returned to the kitchen and arranged the eggs around the table.

Nicky stood to the side, a dish towel over one arm. "Here are the specials *du jour*," he announced. "Eggs over easy, eggs Benedict, egg salad—"

"Nicky!" cried Claire and Margo.

Mal and Dawn began to laugh. The Pike kids could make anything fun.

12th CHAPTER

"I want a divorce."

"I beg your pardon?" said Mrs Boyden.

"I want to divorce Miles."

It was Shawna Riverson who was speaking, and she wasn't kidding. Our Modern Living class had just got under way, and I had a feeling it wasn't going to be a typical class. What was typical about a class in which the pupils got married and had to care for egg-babies?

When we had settled ourselves at our desks that morning, Mrs Boyden had moved in front of her desk. Usually she sits behind it in a teacher-y sort of way. But on that day, she was wearing jeans and a casual top, and she perched herself *on* her desk.

"Okay, kids, let's talk," she had said. "Tell me how you're doing as couples. Tell me how each of you is doing as half of a couple."

That was when Shawna had said she wanted a divorce.

"Shawna, what's going on?" asked Mrs Boyden.

"It's just not working out, that's all," she said.

A couple of kids sniggered. Shawna sounded as if she were speaking lines from a soap opera. Logan and I looked at each other. *We* weren't sniggering. We hadn't laughed much since the night at the cinema. If something was wrong between Shawna and Miles, I could understand that. These things happened.

Mrs Boyden didn't laugh, of course. She gazed solemnly at Shawna. "Tell me what's happening," she said.

"I have to take complete charge of the — of our baby." (Apparently, Shawna and Miles had not named their child.) "Miles hardly ever takes care of it. I lug it around school. I do everything."

Mrs Boyden didn't so much as glance at Miles. She never turned her attention away from Shawna. "Have you asked him to help?" she wanted to know. "Or do you just expect him to?"

"She just expects me to!" Miles burst out. "She never talks to me. She acts as if I'm a mind reader. As if I'm supposed to know everything she thinks or everything she wants."

"Hold on, Miles," Mrs Boyden interrupted. "Let Shawna finish speaking. Then you can have a turn. Shawna?"

"Well, I shouldn't have to *ask* him to do everything."

"Has he ever taken care of a baby before?" asked Mrs Boyden.

"I don't know."

"No, I haven't!" exclaimed Miles.

"But the point is, I have this egg all the time," said Shawna. Yesterday I missed half my gym class moving the—the baby around, trying to keep it out of the sun. And I was late for school this morning because I left the egg at home and had to go back for it."

"I see," said Mrs Boyden. "Miles?"

While Miles spoke, I thought. Shawna and Miles hadn't named their egg. They didn't want to be bothered with it. As far as Shawna was concerned, having a baby was a pain in the neck. Yet Shawna did treat the egg as her baby. If she'd been totally disinterested, she could have left her baby at home that morning when she realized what she'd done. But she went back for it. I was amazed by how real our children had become to us. On some level, my classmates and I felt as if we were actually married and as if we were actually parents. Mrs Boyden was pretty clever. Maybe she was a little unconventional, but she was becoming one of my favourite teachers.

"I don't really have time for the egg or for this experiment," Miles was saying, "but I wouldn't, you know, abandon a kid. I'd take care of the egg, if Shawna would ever give it to me."

"Why haven't you ever asked for it?" exploded Shawna. Her eyes had filled with tears. By then, the room was absolutely silent. No one was sniggering. No one was even smiling.

Miles looked at his hands, which were folded on his desk. His mumbled answer to Shawna was, "I don't know."

Shawna didn't reply. She turned her head away in disgust.

That was when Logan poked me. I leaned towards him, thinking he was going to whisper something about Shawna. Instead, he pointed across the room to two kids I didn't know very well, Angela and Kevin. They were holding hands and Angela was crying. In the emptiness that seemed to follow Miles's statement, Angela put up her hand (the one that wasn't clinging to Kevin).

"Yes, Angela?" said Mrs Boyden. She handed Angela a box of Kleenex but didn't tell her to stop crying or anything.

I was completely unprepared for what Angela said. I'd thought she was crying because of what had gone on between Shawna and Miles. Maybe they reminded her of her own parents. But when Angela said, "Um, Kevin and I lost our baby," I nearly died.

"What do you mean?" asked Mrs Boyden.

"We lost her."

"We lost the *egg*," Kevin spoke up. "It happened yesterday afternoon. We were at the park. Cathy was with us. She's our egg. I mean, she was our egg. And she was in the box we always kept her in."

"The yellow biscuit tin," Angela added.

"Right," said Kevin. "Cathy was with us when we left school, and she was with us when we reached the park. We checked. But when we were leaving the park, we checked again, and the box was empty."

"We tried to retrace our steps," said Angela. "We walked around everywhere. But we couldn't find her."

"We don't know how she got out of the box."

"I feel terrible," said Angela. "Honestly. I mean, if she really had been our kid . . . How could we have been so irresponsible?" Angela was crying again.

The room was silent. I suppose everyone was thinking similar thoughts. That in the blink of an eye, anything can happen to a child. You turn around and she's gone— lost or maybe even kidnapped. Or she's eaten something poisonous. Or she's fallen,

105

or been hit by a car. Those things happen every day to all kinds of families.

Angela and Kevin were the first kids in our Modern Living class to lose their baby, and it wasn't funny.

"Are you worried about the grade you'll get on your project now?" asked Mrs Boyden, which seemed a little insensitive.

"No!" cried Angela. (She shouted it, actually.)

At the same time, Kevin said, "Yeah, I suppose so."

Angela gave him a hard look, then softened. "All right, I suppose I am a little worried, but that wasn't the first thing I thought about when I looked in the box and discovered it empty."

Mrs Boyden nodded. "I understand. Listen, don't worry about your grade. You still owe me a paper, and you can complete it despite what has happened, but some aspects of your project will now change. See me after class, okay?"

"Okay," answered Kevin and Angela.

Mrs Boyden turned her attention to the rest of the class. "What else?" she asked. She propped her feet on an empty chair. "Anyone? No one? . . . So things are perfect for the rest of you?"

At that point, I nearly put up my hand. No, things were not just fine between

Logan and me. We had nearly lost our own child. We had discovered we didn't quite trust one another as parents.

"Mrs Boyden?" said a quiet voice.

I turned round. The voice belonged to a boy who was new at school. He'd been paired up with this girl called Zoe.

"Yes, Tarik?" said Mrs Boyden.

Tarik couldn't look at our teacher. He couldn't look at Zoe or anyone else, either. He stared straight ahead and sort of spoke to the blackboard. "Maybe I should talk to you about this after class, but I—I can't complete the project. I've never had to say that to a teacher before, but it's the truth. I can't do this."

"Why not?" asked Mrs Boyden gently.

"It's just . . . too much. I mean, Zoe—she's doing her part. But, see, I play two sports and I'm in the choir and I have an after-school job, and my parents are getting divorced and my mum needs a lot of help and I can't do this egg thing, too."

"You mean, caring for a child is more than you can handle at this point in your life? You're overwhelmed?"

"Well, yeah."

"That's okay. Put that in your paper. There is no expected outcome for this project, nothing right or wrong that can be said in your papers. But I'd like to talk to you after class, too. Zoe as well. We'll work something out. Okay. Anyone else?"

Whew! What a class. When it was over, Logan and I just sat in our chairs. Logan doodled. I looked at Sammie, safe in her basket on Logan's desk, protected by more padding than ever.

"I suppose we aren't the only ones having problems," I said.

"I suppose not," replied Logan. "In fact, I think we're doing pretty well."

"I bet most parents argue about how to bring up their kids."

"Not to mention other things. Like money. My parents had a big loud talk about money last night. That's what they call arguments—loud talks. And they had the loud talk at about two A.M."

"Scary," I commented.

"Yeah." Logan got to his feet. He picked up Sammie's basket."

"I thought you had baseball practice for gym today," I said.

"I do."

"So let me take Sammie."

"Well—"

"You still don't trust me, do you? Just because I lost her for five seconds. Logan, accidents happen. Look at Kevin and Angela."

"I know." Logan didn't let go of Sammie, though.

My eyes filled with tears. "I'll see you later," I whispered, and ran out of the room without Sammie.

"Mary Anne!" called Logan.

I didn't answer.

Logan and I had a long way to go before we could reconcile our differences.

13th
CHAPTER

Not long after that memorable Modern Living class, I found myself babysitting for Ricky and Rose again. For some reason, I wasn't looking forward to the job. I wasn't dreading it; I just wasn't approaching it with glee. I wasn't jumping up and down, singing, "Oh, boy, babies! I get to take care of babies again!"

Luckily, Sammie didn't come along on the job with me. Logan had taken her home with him.

"This will make the afternoon much easier," I said to Kristy, as we left school that day. "Just *two* babies."

"Yeah. Piece of cake. Sitting for the Rodowsky boys could be much harder. The Walking Disaster and his two brothers. Think what could happen at the Rodowskys' in an afternoon."

I rolled my eyes. "Mayhem," I said. "Chaos. Anarchy."

Kristy smiled. "Oh, there's my bus!" she cried. "I've got to go. Have fun this afternoon, Mary Anne."

"Thanks!" I said. "I'll talk to you tonight."

I walked to the Salems' house, dawdling a little. The weather was absolutely gorgeous, warmer than usual, with a wonderful smell of damp earth and new leaves in the air. Perfect baby-walking weather.

I rang the Salems' bell and was greeted by Mrs Salem, who looked pretty worn out. Her eyes were red, and she seemed limp.

"Hi, Mary Anne," she said. "Whew! I'm exhausted. The last thing I want to do is go to this meeting, but I'm on the board of the Small Animal Rescue League, so I have to attend."

I hesitated. I wanted to ask Mrs Salem if everything was okay, but I wasn't sure I should. I mean, adults always ask kids that question, but should a kid ask an adult? I didn't want Mrs Salem to think I was being nosy. However, *she* had said she was exhausted, so I went ahead and asked.

"Oh, I'm fine," Mrs Salem replied. "Just tired. The babies seem to be changing their routine. I never know what to expect. They were sleeping through the night just fine, and now, well, they're not. And they didn't go down for their naps this afternoon until later than usual. So they should sleep longer. You'll probably have a chance to get some homework done this afternoon."

"Great. I was going to take Rose and Ricky for a walk, but I *do* have a lot of work."

Mrs Salem wrote down the number of the Small Animal Rescue League and reminded me where the emergency numbers could be found. Then she left. I watched her back her car down the drive. She was yawning.

I settled myself at the kitchen table with a glass of orange juice and a bran muffin. I opened the book of short stories we were reading for English class.

" '*The Telltale Heart*,' by Edgar Allan Poe," I murmured.

The story was scary. I don't know why I was surprised. Poe's stories are all scary. I was reading along, and my heart was beginning to pound, when something squeaked.

I yelped and knocked over the glass of orange juice.

"Drat!" I cried, as the juice spread across the Salems' table and dripped down one of the legs and onto the floor.

I mopped it up with paper towels and forgot about the squeak until . . .

"WAHH!"

I jumped, jerking my hands up and knocking the book across the kitchen to a work surface, where it landed on this bowl of fruit.

"WAHH!" I heard again. It was Ricky. I could tell his cry from Rose's. I could also tell that his cry was going to become a scream.

I ran upstairs and into the twins' room. Ricky was sitting in his cot. His face was red and tearstained.

"Hey, Ricky. What's the matter?" I said soothingly as I lifted him into my arms. "Your mum said you just went off to sleep. Why are you up so soon? Are you wet? Or hungry?"

Ricky's answer was a shriek, so I hurried him out of the room before he could wake his sister.

I carried Ricky to the kitchen.

I felt his nappy. Dry.

I offered him a bottle. He fussed and turned his head away.

"What is it? What can I do for you?" I asked.

Ricky drooled and cried.

From upstairs, I thought I heard a whimper, although it was hard to hear over the noise Ricky was making.

"Come on," I said to him. "We'd better check on Rose."

I carried Ricky back upstairs. With every

step, his wails seemed to grow louder. "Shh, shh," I said soothingly. "Calm down."

But he didn't. By the time we had reached the bedroom, he was throwing his head back and screaming so hard I thought he would choke.

Rose stirred in the cot. Her eyelids fluttered. She was waking up.

I fled downstairs. "Ricky, Rose needs her sleep. Can't you calm down?" I said. I walked him around the ground floor of the house, making a circle from the kitchen to the dining room to the living room, through the hall, and back into the kitchen. As long as I kept moving, Ricky confined his crying to loud whimpers. If I slowed down, the screaming started. I knew what he needed. He needed a walk in the buggy. I was pretty sure that (and only that) would calm him down. But what about Rose? I couldn't wake her up just because her brother needed a walk. I also couldn't check on her while her brother was crying. If I brought him with me, he'd disturb her. If I left him strapped into his high chair or his baby chair, he would begin the awful ear-shattering, choking screaming.

I was desperate.

I phoned my sister.

"Dawn, can you come over to the Salems' straight away?" I asked shakily.

"Of course. What's wrong?"

I explained as quickly as I could. "So the thing is," I finished up, "I can't be in two places at the same time. Someone has to take Ricky outside. I've never heard such screaming. Or seen such drooling."

"I bet he's teething," said Dawn. "Give him one of those hard crackers. I'll be over as soon as I can."

"Thank you. You've saved my life," I said seriously.

Fifteen minutes later, Dawn arrived at the Salems', sweaty from having ridden her bicycle in such a hurry. I was still walking Ricky in circles around the ground floor. He was gumming madly on a teething biscuit I'd found in the kitchen cupboard. The biscuit had calmed him down slightly—as long as we kept moving.

"Do you mind taking Ricky?" I asked Dawn. I circled from the dining room into the living room, Dawn at my heels. "I'd take him, but I think I'd better stay here in case Mrs Salem comes home. It would probably be better if she found the same babysitter who was here when she left the house."

"I don't mind taking him," Dawn replied. "It's so nice out. Where's the buggy? We'll leave straight away."

"It's in the garage. Can you wheel it to the front door? I don't want to stop moving until I can put Ricky straight into the buggy."

Dawn found the buggy while I circled with Ricky. As soon as she was waiting outside, I made one last circle, but when I reached the hall, I turned right instead of left, walked through the front door, which Dawn was holding open, and plopped Ricky in the buggy. Dawn was pushing him down the walk before he knew what was happening. Immediately, his cries began to fade.

I went back inside and checked on Rose, who was (miraculously) still sleeping. Then I collapsed in an armchair in the living room.

I was just reclining there, enjoying the peace when . . .

"WAHH!"

Oh, no. Not again.

I ran upstairs.

Now Rose was awake, sitting up in her cot, screaming and drooling.

"I suppose you're teething, too," I said wearily, understanding why Mrs Salem looked so haggard. "At least I know what to do now. You need a biscuit and a walk."

I found a teething biscuit for Rose—and then realized that in order to take her for a walk, I needed the buggy, of course. I ran to the front door and looked up and down the street. Dawn and Ricky had already disappeared. Double drat. So I picked up Crying Baby Number Two and began making the circle. Kitchen to dining room to living room to hall and back to kitchen.

I was still walking Rose when Dawn returned, and Dawn and I were still walking both babies when Mrs Salem returned.

"Do I *have* to write about that job in the notebook?" I asked Dawn that evening. "I would really rather forget the entire incident."

14th CHAPTER

Ordinarily, when the phone rings at our house, everyone runs for it as if we were going to win a prize for being the first one to answer. On the evening after my latest disaster with Ricky and Rose, the phone rang, and *no one* dived for it.

We were all tired.

I was tired from my taxing afternoon. Dawn was tired for the same reason. And Dad and Sharon were tired because they'd each had a difficult day at work. Every member of my family was worn out in a different room.

Ring . . . ring . . . ring.

The phone rang three times before I realized what was happening.

"Dawn, can you get that?" I called from my bedroom.

"Why?" she called from *her* bedroom.

"Because it's *ring*ing."

118

"Mum'll get it."

"No she won't!" Sharon yelled from downstairs. "She's too tired."

Ring . . . ring.

"Will someone please answer the phone?" said Dad.

"Mary Anne will!" shouted Dawn.

"I will not! I can't move!"

The phone stopped ringing.

"Did someone answer that?" called Sharon.

"No!" replied Dad and Dawn and I.

"You know, that could have been an important call," said Dawn. "Maybe someone died and left us an island or something."

"A tropical island?" I asked.

"Yes, with palm trees and beautiful seashells."

The phone rang again.

I sprinted into Dad and Sharon's room. So did Dawn. We grabbed the receiver at the same time. "Hello?" we said.

"Hello?" said Dad and Sharon on the other extension.

"Hello," said a fifth voice.

"Logan?" I asked.

"Mary Anne?"

"Okay, everyone can get off the phone," I said. "We haven't inherited an island. This is just Logan calling."

"*Just* Logan?" he repeated. "Thanks a lot."

"Don't be insulted," I told him, giggling, as the rest of my family went back to being tired. "It's just that— Oh, never mind. It's a long story."

"Oh. Well, I was phoning because . . . You won't believe this, but good news! Sammie is walking, and I captured the event on video-tape."

I began to laugh again. "A Kodak moment?" I suggested.

"Definitely." Logan was laughing, too.

I knew he was phoning so we could talk things over, so we could make up once and for all. "How is Sammie really?" I asked.

"She's fine. How were the twins this afternoon?"

"A mess. They're teething. I'm glad you were looking after Sammie today. I could *never* have handled her *and* the twins. As it was, Dawn had to come over and help me."

"Wow! I hardly ever hear you say you can't handle a sitting job."

"Sitting is different when babies are involved."

"Yeah. Mary Anne? I'm sorry we've been arguing."

"Me, too," I answered. "It's Sammie and Modern Living. That's why we're arguing. Mrs Boyden is asking us to do something really difficult—be adults, be married, have babies, and at the same time be kids at school. I'm glad she didn't give us *real* babies. Can you imagine what a state we'd be in now?"

"For one thing, we'd be broke. Dad took Hunter to the doctor for a check-up the other day, and you know what that visit cost? Seventy-five dollars! Seventy-five dollars when nothing was wrong with him in the first place. And we still haven't got the bill from the lab for the tests they're doing. Who knows how much that will be for? I don't know how my parents can afford to look after three children. Kerry and Hunter and I are ex*pen*sive!"

"Well, we already know we can't afford even an egg right now, but I didn't expect us to argue so much. I thought that when two people got married they just moved into a nice little place and began hanging curtains and planting flower beds."

"You mean they played house?"

"I suppose so. I never thought about stuff like what to do if you can't find a babysitter. Or if you and your husband couldn't agree on how to bring up a baby."

"Maybe when you're older you can work those things out more easily."

"Maybe. I don't think that being older solves everything, though. Look at Dawn's mother and father. Or Kristy's mother and father. Or Stacey's mother and father."

"Yeah. But I bet you have a better *chance*

at a relationship if you wait a while. Until after college or something."

"Probably."

"I mean, we couldn't get married now," said Logan.

"We? You and *I*? Get married *now*?" I squeaked. "I'll say we couldn't. I want to enjoy the rest of the eighth grade first. I want to enjoy being thirteen and not have to worry about all those things I'll have plenty of time to worry about when I'm twenty-two or something."

"Yeah. I would like to play baseball without first having to think of who's going to watch Sammie. That would be a luxury. I'm not ready for so many complications."

"Me, neither. Logan, I really like you. I hope you know that."

"I do."

"But I'm not ready to be your wife, or anyone's else's wife."

"That's cool. I'm not ready to be a husband."

"Do you think this is the kind of material Mrs Boyden wants us to include in our report? What we learned about ourselves?"

"Probably. I think she wants us to consider ourselves as couples and also as the single parts of couples. Remember the questions she asked at the beginning of class one day? The day Shawna said she wanted to divorce Miles?"

"Yeah. And we've learned some things

about loyalty and trust and independence and responsibility. Maybe we should divide our paper into two sections. In one, we'll describe what we've learned about ourselves. In the other, we'll describe what we've learned about relationships; about the aspects of relationships."

"That's a great idea," agreed Logan. He sighed.

"What's wrong?" I asked.

"Nothing. I'm just sitting here looking at Sammie. When this project is over, I'll miss her."

"Me, too."

"But not *too* much."

"No, not *too* much." I paused. "I wonder what Mrs Boyden will do with our babies when we don't need them any more."

"I don't even want to think about it."

"Neither do I. I think I should go now, Logan. I haven't started my homework yet. But I'll see you and Sammie at school tomorrow."

"Okay. 'Bye, Mary Anne. Love you."

"Love you, too."

We hung up. I was heading for my room but detoured down the hall to Dawn's room instead. I walked in and sat in her armchair.

"What did Logan want?" asked Dawn. She was sitting at her desk, writing up a lab report for science class, but she stopped and looked at me. She stuck her pencil in the pencil jar.

"To talk about Sammie. Nothing special, though. You know what I've been thinking, Dawn?"

"What?"

"About the Kumbel catalogue. You can throw it away."

"I can? How come?"

"Well, what's *your* opinion about my dad and your mum having a baby now? I mean, what's your opinion since you spent the afternoon with a fussing, teething baby?"

"Oh." Dawn looked sheepish.

"Because *I* was thinking," I went on, "that maybe it isn't a very good idea after all. Not that *we* couldn't take care of a baby properly. We *are* professional babysitters. But a new baby might be rough on our parents at their age. Not that they're old—"

"Of course not," interrupted Dawn. "But they might not be strong enough to go through teething."

"Or to toilet train a kid."

"Anyhow, they need their sleep now. How could they get up every three hours during the night to feed a newborn?"

"They couldn't. And in about ten years the kid would want to go to Disney World. Do you think Dad would ride Space Mountain with our brother or sister?"

"No way. Mum probably wouldn't, either."

"And you and I would be out of college

and living on our own by then," I pointed out. "So we wouldn't be any help."

"That's right."

"Where *is* the Kumbel catalogue?" I asked.

Dawn found it in her wardrobe. We opened it to the baby pages we had marked, and we gazed at the pictures.

"Not having a baby will save a lot of money, too," I said, looking at the prices. Baby equipment was not cheap.

"But that little lamp *is* awfully cute," said Dawn wistfully.

"Well, save your pennies," I said. "Maybe one day you can buy it for your own room." Dawn closed the catalogue. I stood up. "I'm still curious to know what our baby brother or sister would have looked like."

"And I think it would have been great if our parents had had a baby of their own. A little Schafer-Spier."

"But I suppose it wasn't meant to be."

"I suppose not."

15th CHAPTER

It was the last session of our Modern Living class. The following week we would begin a new course—Health. No one was very interested in it, but we had to take it, so complaining was no good. (Miles tried to look on the bright side. "Isn't sex education part of Health?" I heard him say. Logan laughed. I blushed.)

Logan and I walked into Mrs Boyden's class together. I was carrying Sammie in her basket. Logan was holding our precious term paper. It was 32 pages long, typed, single-spaced. Well, actually, word-processed, not typed. Logan had printed it out on his home computer.

We took our seats, and I put Sammie on my desk. Logan and I watched the room fill up with our classmates and their eggs. Mrs Boyden was at her desk, thumbing through her lesson book. When the bell rang, she closed the book and stood up.

"Well," she began, smiling, "you've made it. You survived."

"*We* didn't," said Angela. "Kevin and I lost Cathy. We—"

"I meant you survived as married couples," Mrs Boyden replied gently. "And I'm proud of all of you. Some very heavy issues have been discussed in this class, along with some very personal feelings. Your honesty is what made the class a success. Also, your ability to suspend disbelief. If you hadn't been able to pretend your eggs were babies, you wouldn't have learned so much.

"Today," Mrs Boyden went on, "I would like each husband and wife to pair up and write a short composition, which will be handed in with your final papers. The subject of the composition is saying goodbye to your children. The time is now twenty-one years in the future. Your babies have grown up, become adults, and finished their schooling. They are ready to leave you and lead lives of their own."

"Logan," I whispered, feeling tearful, "Sammie doesn't need us any more. She's going to leave us!"

"At the end of the class," said Mrs Boyden, "you will leave your eggs behind. They will no longer be your responsibility."

"What are you going to do with them?" asked Shawna.

"Do you really want to know?"

Shawna shook her head. "I don't think so."

"Okay. Break up into your pairs, then."

I slid my desk over to Logan's desk, bringing Sammie with me.

"So?" said Logan. "Where's Sammie going?"

"Off to her first important job," I answered. "In New York." (New York is where I hope to land *my* first important job.)

"We're going to let our baby move to big, dangerous New York City?"

"Dear, she's not a baby any more," I reminded my husband. "She's an adult. She's twenty-one. And she's been offered a position in a publishing house. She will be an editorial assistant. We can't hold her back."

"You're right," agreed Logan.

We wrote our composition and added it to our paper.

After we had handed in our work, I looked at Sammie and said, "I suppose this is goodbye. You've been a real—"

"A real good egg?" Logan interrupted.

I made a face at him. But I didn't say anything. I knew he was joking around because he didn't want to get sentimental in class, where everyone could see him. Some men have such a hard time dealing with their emotions.

That afternoon our BSC meeting was attended by seven humans and no eggs. Although earlier I had been sad about letting Sammie go off to New York, I was now feeling quite free. I wasn't the only one.

Stacey bounced into club headquarters crying, "Freedom at last!" She sounded the way most kids do on the day the summer holidays start. "No more mixing bowl," she went on, "but I *do* miss Bobby . . . sort of. Well, just a teensy bit."

At 5:28, Jessie ran into the room, the last club member to arrive. As she settled onto the floor next to Mallory, she looked around, then asked, "Where are your babies?"

"Gone," said Kristy sadly.

"They grew up," added Dawn.

"Mine went to New York to start a career," I said.

Jessi and Mal didn't know *what* we were talking about, so we described our last Modern Living class to them.

"Cool. What are the rest of your children doing?" asked Mallory.

"Bobby is going to teach high school history," said Stacey.

"Izzy became a car mechanic," said Kristy. "He opened a garage in Stamford. I made him promise to visit every Sunday."

"My baby is going to become a famous artist," said Claud. "Naturally."

"Mine's at medical school," said Dawn.

The phone rang then, and we arranged a job for Claudia with the Newtons.

"You know what I think?" I spoke up after a break in the conversation. "I suppose if I absolutely *had* to, I could bring up a child of my own. But I wouldn't want to. I'm too young."

"Also, your dad isn't ready to be a grandfather," said Stacey.

"No, I'm serious, Stace. I'm not kidding around. Do you think you could be a parent right now? I mean, if you'd just given birth?"

Stacey frowned. "No. I really don't. How would I support a baby? Anyway, I don't *want* to be a parent. Not yet."

"You're right," I agreed. "I could only bring up a baby if I lived at home and Dawn and Dad and Sharon helped me. I couldn't do it by myself."

"I do want to have kids one day, though," said Dawn.

"Definitely!" agreed the rest of us.

"But maybe when I'm older," she went on. "When I'm twenty-five. Maybe even thirty. You know, now lots of women are having their first baby when they're *forty*. Or older. I'm not in any hurry."

"Me, neither," I said, "but I don't want to wait until I'm forty. Twenty-five sounds like a good age."

"I'm going to have eight children, like my mum did," commented Mal.

"It's a good thing you won't have them all at once," replied Stacey. "You might want to stop after one or two."

"Maybe. Anyway, I don't have to decide now."

"And in two years you'll take Modern Living," said Kristy, "and you can have a trial run with just one egg-baby."

"I hope my first baby is a girl," said Jessi dreamily. "I will call her Mary Rose. I've always wanted a daughter named Mary Rose."

The phone rang again then, and our meeting became busy with BSC stuff. No one mentioned the eggs again.

When Dawn and I got home that evening, we received a call from Sharon, saying she and Dad would be about half an hour late and asking us to start dinner. So we did. As we took things out of the fridge and put them on the kitchen table, Dawn said, "Mary Anne, do you think you'll ever be able to eat eggs again?"

I shook my head. "Not for a long, *long* time."

"I know what you mean."

My sister and I began chopping vegetables for a salad. "I certainly am glad," I said, slicing a carrot, "that we didn't say anything more to our parents about having a baby."

"Whew! I'll say," agreed Dawn.

"Can you imagine if we had convinced them and your mum had got pregnant straight away and then we had finished Modern Living and had changed our minds?"

"We would have been a little late."

"Yeah, just a little."

"Is being a little late like being a little pregnant?" Dawn asked.

I laughed. "I suppose so. Either you are or you aren't."

Dad and Sharon entered the kitchen just in time to hear that last part of our conversation.

"Who's having a baby?" asked Dad suspiciously.

"No one, thank goodness," I answered. "No one we know of."

"How's dinner coming along, girls?" asked Sharon.

"It's ready," I said.

"Let's eat," said Dawn.

"Let's eat in the dining room," added Sharon.

"Ooh, special occasion?" I asked.

Sharon shrugged. "Maybe, maybe not."

We sat at the dining room table and passed around the salad and this Chinese vegetable dish Sharon makes and brown bread and these vegetable patties that are supposed to look like hamburgers but don't.

When our plates were full, Sharon looked at Dawn, then at me, and smiled. "Girls," she said, "Richard and I have been thinking about your wish for a baby. You haven't mentioned it for a while, but we know that doesn't mean you aren't still *think*ing about it."

I know my face turned pale then. I felt faint. Across the table from me, Dawn's eyes widened to the size of basketballs, and her hands began to shake. Oh, *no*. Why couldn't parents just forget things once in a while? Why did they have to remember everything?

"Um," I said.

"Um," said Dawn.

"You see, the thing is, Dawn and I talked about it and we realized we shouldn't have . . ." My voice trailed off.

"Don't worry," said Sharon. "It's okay. Richard and I have discussed everything and we decided if you really want something to care for, you may get another pet. Tigger might like some company."

I let out the breath I was holding. Oh, a

pet. I managed a grin at Dawn, who grinned back. "Do you want a pet?" I asked her.

"Do you?" Dawn countered.

"Not really. Tigger's enough."

"That's how I feel. . . . But thanks, Mum. Thanks, Richard."

"Yeah, thanks," I said.

Dad looked surprised. "We thought you'd jump at the chance to get another pet."

"We might have, if it weren't for Modern Living," I replied.

"Modern Living?"

"Yeah. Dad," I said, "you have no idea how hard it is to be a parent."

Celebrate their 50th Adventure with the Babysitters!

Collect all these personalised Babysitters goodies! Scholastic Children's Books are delighted to bring you this unique limited offer. Send off for your special souvenir keyring, school year diary or roomy tote bag, all featuring your favourite babysitters. Better still, collect all three! Stocks are limited, so be sure and post your coupon off early!

A full colour **Babysitters Club** keyring   99p + 25p p+p   _____

A **Babysitters Club** School Year Diary   £2.99 + £1 p+p   _____

A 100% cotton canvas **Babysitters Club**
tote bag   £3.99 + £1 p+p   _____

Conditions:
1. Where more than one item is ordered, a flat charge of £1 p+p will apply.
2. Where possible, orders will be fulfilled within 28 days; in some instances a delay may occur.
3. Stocks of these items are limited. Where an item cannot be supplied cheques or postal orders will be returned. Scholastic Children's Books recommend an early response to avoid disappointment.

Simply tick the item(s) you would like to receive, and send a cheque or postal order (no cash please) for the full amount plus postage and packing to: Babysitters Souvenir Offer, c/o Scholastic Publications Ltd, Westfield Road, Southam, Warwickshire, CV33 0JH.

Name..

Address..

....

....Postcode...........................

GREEN WATCH by Anthony Masters

BATTLE FOR THE BADGERS
Tim's been sent to stay with his weird Uncle Seb and his two kids, Flower and Brian, who run Green Watch – an environmental pressure group. At first Tim thinks they're a bunch of cranks – but soon he finds himself battling to save badgers from extermination . . .

SAD SONG OF THE WHALE
Tim leaps at the chance to join Green Watch on an anti-whaling expedition. But soon, he and the other members of Green Watch, find themselves shipwrecked and fighting for their lives . . .

DOLPHIN'S REVENGE
The members of Green Watch are convinced that Sam Jefferson is mistreating his dolphins – but how can they prove it? Not only that, but they must save Loner, a wild dolphin, from captivity . . .

MONSTERS ON THE BEACH
The Green Watch team is called to investigate a suspected radiation leak. Teddy McCormack claims to have seen mutated crabs and sea-plants, but there's no proof, and Green Watch don't know whether he's crazy or there's been a cover-up . . .

GORILLA MOUNTAIN
Tim, Brian and Flower fly to Africa to meet the Bests, who are protecting gorillas from poachers. But they are ambushed and Alison Best is kidnapped. It is up to them to rescue her *and* save the gorillas . . .

SPIRIT OF THE CONDOR
Green Watch has gone to California on a surfing holiday – but not for long! Someone is trying to kill the Californian Condor, the bird cherished by an Indian tribe – the Daiku – and without which the tribe will die. Green Watch must struggle to save both the Condor and the Daiku . . .